THE CLIQUE

SUMMER COLLECTION

ALICIA

THE CLIQUE
SUMMER COLLECTION
ALICIA

A CLIQUE NOVEL BY
LISI HARRISON

poppy

LITTLE, BROWN AND COMPANY
New York   Boston

Poppy

Little, Brown and Company
Hachette Book Group USA
237 Park Avenue, New York, NY 10017
For more of your favorite series, go to www.pickapoppy.com

First Edition: June 2008

The Poppy name and logo are trademarks of Hachette Book Group USA.

Cover design by Andrea C. Uva
Cover photo by Roger Moenks
Author photo by Gillian Crane

alloy**entertainment**

Produced by Alloy Entertainment
151 West 26th Street, New York, NY 10001

ISBN: 978-0-316-02753-3

10 9 8 7 6 5 4 3 2 1
CWO
Printed in the United States of America

For my mom, who taught me what being there for someone really means.

Alicia Rivera stuffed her purple and turquoise vintage Pucci silk wrap in the side pocket of her Louis Vuitton monogrammed carry-on and wheeled it toward the baggage claim. She could practically *hear* her mother scolding her for treating the delicate, wrinkle-prone fabric with such reckless abandon. But she opposite of cared. Nadia was back in Westchester, and Alicia had just arrived in Spain. Thanks to an all-consuming lipo-gone-wrong trial, her attorney father and supportive mother had to stay home. And that meant *she* was parent-free for the first summer of her entire life.

The rules were about to change.

Barcelona International Airport (or *Bar-theh-lona,* as the locals called it) was another reminder that Alicia was a world away from New York. Women whizzed past her, smelling like musky cologne and wearing brightly colored pumps. Men wore hair gel that shined like MAC Lipglass, and loafers without socks. College kids with bulging neon backpacks that had been sloppily stitched with American or Canadian flags shuffled by in Tevas, their expressions a mix of airplane-groggy and let-the-games-begin psyched.

If Massie had been in the overly air-conditioned terminal,

she'd have been rolling her eyes at the "poor-taste parade." But Alicia had a secret appreciation for the variety. Light denim washes and sneakers that looked like bowling shoes weren't exactly her thing, but they were different—a welcome change from the usual Rock & Republic five-pockets and Havaianas. And isn't that what summer's all about?

A loud, girly squeal, the kind perfected by *High School Musical* fans, forced Alicia's attention to the orange wall of billboards to her left. Between the faded ads for a Goya exhibit at El Prado and some sugary cereal made of red marshmallow-shaped bulls were five Euro-tweens giggle-posing next to a poster of an overly Photoshopped, deeply bronzed, black-haired, hazel-eyed boy.

After their picture had been taken, they each kissed his bleached, bathroom-tile-like teeth, leaving behind cherry red lip prints and a citrus-floral medley of the different perfumes they must have been sampling in the duty-free shop.

Alicia stopped in front of the billboard and tried to decipher the yellow, all-caps font that shouted: SI ERES UNA VER-DADERA BELLEZA ESPAÑOLA TE QUIERO PARA MI PROXIMO VIDEO MUSICAL. EL BAILE RECREADO PARA LA CANCIÓN "RAIN IN SPAIN." LAS AUDICIONES SERAN EN EL HOTEL LINDO. ¡I! TE HARE UNA ESTRELLA.

Alicia had learned enough Spanish from her mother and their six previous visits to know that the pop star on the poster was looking for "a real Spanish beauty" to be in his "new music video." And—from what she could gather—his name was ¡i!.

Instantly, a vision of herself in a swiveling makeup chair being blushed, blow-dried, then whisked off to wardrobe made Alicia's travel-chapped hands slick with excitement-sweat. After the Spanish paparazzi had made her a household name, she'd return to U.S. soil, ready to claim her seat on the alpha throne. She'd hold a private viewing party in her father's screening room, where the Pretty Committee and their new crushes (TBD) would admire her on the big screen as she played her international music video for them over and over and over. Every time she'd turn it off, they'd beg her to run it again so they could admire her beauty and study her advanced dance moves one more time. It would be the perfect way to start the eighth grade. Massie would envy her times ten. And *that* would give her a surplus of confidence that would fuel her until Thanksgiving, if not a week or two longer.

So what if she wasn't a *real* Spanish beauty. Her mother was, and that made her half. And *half* of Alicia was better than anyone else's whole—at least from what she could see in the Barcelona International Airport: Her slick dark hair was the shiniest, her white Diors were the roundest, her navy Ralph Lauren shirtdress and wide gold metallic belt were the most stylish, and her wood-soled Miu Miu wedges were the highest. Besides, she trained at Westchester's prestigious Body Alive Dance Studio. And there wasn't a purebred in all of Spain who could claim that.

She might not have been an alpha yet, but becoming a Spalpha—a Spanish alpha—was totally doable. And once she ruled Spain for a summer, she'd have enough experience to dominate Octavian Country Day School back home. From the moment Alicia stepped off the plane, twenty-seven people—wait, make that twenty-eight—had checked her out. And she hadn't even arrived at baggage claim yet.

When she did, she spotted her sixteen-year-old twin cousins, Celia and Isobel Callas. They were sitting in one of those long golf carts used to transport luggage and old people, teasing the driver by repeatedly knocking off his black patent-leather cap. They threw their long, tanned necks back and cackled as he feigned frustration. It probably wasn't every day—or every decade, even—that the pint-size porter had two leggy, raven-haired socialites ravage him for free. The scene made Alicia's exfoliated feet tingle with joy.

"Yippeeee!" Celia—or was it Isobel?—hollered as she tossed the driver's cap like a Frisbee. It landed on the moving luggage conveyor belt and began making its circular journey. He rolled his eyes playfully and hopped off the cart to chase after it. Isobel—or was it Celia?—jumped in the front seat, gripped the wheel, slammed her metallic gold espadrille on the gas, and began doing donuts across the shiny beige marble floor.

Alicia couldn't have been more proud to call them family.

"*A-lee-cia! A-lee-cia!*" they shouted, speeding toward her.

"*Hola!*" Alicia beam-waved, then jumped out of the way. They screech-stopped in front of her, leaped out, and planted a series of double-cheek welcome kisses on her blushing face.

"So great to see you, Cousin," said Celia, tugging the massive gold C on her massive gold chain. It hung below her barely-there cleavage and knocked against the stiff edges of her fuchsia denim vest. She wore it with a burnt orange taffeta bubble skirt and lace-up gold sandals. Her hair was slicked into a tight bun that reflected more light than the porter's patent-leather cap. "Don't you look very stylish."

"Grassy," Alicia chirped, putting her new abbreviation for *gracias* straight to work.

"I love how you say *grassy*! May I borrow?" asked Isobel, who was wearing a Mediterranean blue tube top, white short shorts, and oversize Ray-Bans with bright blue plastic frames.

They made those?

"*You* can borrow 'grassy,' Iso—I want to borrow that gold belt." Celia reached out and poked Alicia's braided Ralph Lauren.

"Given." Alicia smiled, thinking of her new summer wardrobe and how much her cousins were going to worship it. "My closet is your closet, but . . ." Her voice trailed off as she remembered their thirteen-year-old sister, Nina, and her passion for stealing designer clothes.

The Spanish Loser Beyond Repair had spent a couple weeks at OCD last semester and had not only tried to steal the Pretty Committee's boyfriends but also half the girls' wardrobes. So far there was no sign of her. Alicia crossed her French-mani'd fingers and prayed it would stay that way for the entire summer. With any luck, Nina had been shipped off to a reform school for kleptomaniacs, because there was nothing less Spalpha than a SLBR tagalong with theft issues.

A loud, New York Stock Exchange–type bell rang; then bags started to appear on the conveyor belt. One by one they floated by like pageant contestants, sporting pink bows, plaid scarves, and neon tags to ensure they'd be safely reunited with their loving owners. But no one turned to claim them. Instead, the weary travelers could not take their eyes off the three dark beauties and their bright summer clothes. Already Alicia could feel her Spalpha stock rising.

Isobel lifted her blue Ray-Bans, narrowed her almond-shaped brown eyes, and turned to Celia. She said something quickly in Spanish to her sister. Alicia only managed to pick up the words *borrow, cousin,* and *audition.* Determined to make this a no-secrets summer, she spoke up:

"Are you talking about the video audition?" she asked, proud that she was already in the know.

"*Sí.*" Isobel lowered her voice and her glasses.

"Your American clothes will be perfect." Celia poked the Ralph Lauren belt again.

"I heart that." Alicia rocked back and forth on the wooden heels of her Miu Mius. She felt beautiful and bouncy, like her entire body was made of Pantene-commercial hair. "And maybe I can try out in some of your—"

"You can't!" Celia snapped, her gold necklace swinging back and forth. "You are not true Spanish."

"Puh-lease!" Alicia rolled her tired brown eyes. It was bad enough when Massie called her Fannish (fake Spanish) just because her father, Len, was American. But it was quite another thing to hear it from her own flesh and blood. And no self-respecting alpha would stand for it. The old Alicia would have admitted defeat and resigned herself to a summer of cheering on her cousins while she envy-watched from the sidelines. But the new Alicia was going to fight for her rightful place in the Spalpha kingdom. And she was going to win.

"They asked for a true Spanish beauty, right?" Alicia pressed.

The twins nodded, barely noticing as the porter sneaked up behind them, reclaimed his cart, and sped off.

"Well, what I don't have in *Spanish,* I make up for in *beauty.*" Alicia tossed her hair. She was acting the part now—soon she would become it.

"Point," Isobel nodded, still using Alicia's expression from last summer.

"I say we sneak out of the house tonight and go to the Hotel Lindo. We will party there and search for ¡¡! and his entourage and—"

Sluuuurppppppp. Sluuurrrrppppppp.

The sound of someone straw-draining the last drops of liquid from a glass bottle put an instant hold on their scheme session. Alicia turned to see why and came face-to-face with Nina, who had been lurking behind her, an empty Orangina in hand. She was still tall and thin. Her boobs were still massive. But she no longer posed a physical threat, thanks to her new hair-*don't*. She sported thick platinum bangs, and a Dora the Explorer bob grazed her rounded jaw. On a supermodel in New York who only wore skinny jeans, tight black turtlenecks, and matte red lipstick, this look would have been hawt. But on someone wearing a ketchup-stained turquoise racer-back tank with yellow linen pants, it came off more like a dare.

"*Hola*," Nina hissed, offering no embrace. She was obviously still bitter that the Pretty Committee had publicly busted her at the OCD Valentine's Day dance for stealing their stuff and asked the police to escort her directly to the airport.

"*Hola*," Alicia responded coldly. In the split second since Nina had appeared, it seemed like everyone who had been watching them turned away. She was terrible for business.

"I know what you were talking about." Nina rubbed her heavily lined brown eyes like she'd just woken up, smudging blue kohl under her bottom lashes. "No one has ever seen ii! in person. What makes you think—"

"Go get Cousin's bags." Celia stomped her gold sandal. "*¡Vamos!* Papa is waiting in the car."

Nina chucked her bottle in a metal trash can and stormed off to retrieve the only set of Louis Vuitton suitcases in the mix.

Isobel leaned in toward Alicia, surrounding her in the unmistakably sunny scent of Bobbi Brown's Beach. "We must not let her know what we are up to. She is a—how you say . . . uh, tagalong! And will make us look bad in front of ii!. If you want to have fun with us this summer, you must avoid Little Sister."

"Done!" Alicia beamed, relieved that they were all thinking the same thing.

"Ready?" Nina asked, wheeling two brown and gold suitcases, one in each hand. She led the way through the sliding glass door outside to the pickup area.

The day was humid and bright. The foreign smell of cigarette smoke and exhaust fumes wafted around them, reminding Alicia that she was entering an alternate universe where anything was possible. Smoking in public was acceptable. Betas could become alphas. Fannish could become Spanish. And Nina and her "rob hobby" could be easily avoided.

Suddenly, Nina stopped walking. She turned around and smiled her toothy Emma Roberts grin at Alicia. "Did my sisters tell you we're sharing a room this summer?"

Celia and Isobel quickly turned to face each other, as if they were deeply involved in a telepathic conversation that couldn't be interrupted.

Alicia's heart thumped to the beat of the salsa music blaring from a blue Mini Cooper that had just whizzed past them. "What do you mean? I always get my own—"

"Mama is renovating the guest wing." Nina licked her puffy lips with delight. "So we will all be together. You, me, my graphic novel collection, and your precious American clothes." She cracked her knuckles as if loosening her fingers for an *Ocean's 11*–size heist.

"Wait! *What?*" Alicia checked her pink, crocodile-strap Gucci watch, wondering if there was time to catch the last flight back to JFK.

Just then, Nina rolled one of the suitcases through a steaming brown clump of . . . "Uh-oh, *perro* poo!"

Everyone stopped to examine the stinky wheel.

Celia and Isobel gasped while Alicia buried her face in her hands, knowing exactly how her poor Louis felt.

"Grassy," Alicia wave-thanked her dashing Uncle Fabian as she stepped out of his black-on-black Escalade. Behind her, Nina, Isobel, and Celia tumbled from the backseat onto the crushed-stone driveway.

"De nada!" he called, pulling the car into a seven-car, climate-controlled garage.

"Welcome!" Marina Callas yell-waved from the wood doorway of the stucco-and-red-tiled estate. Alicia's aunt Marina was five-eight, deeply tanned, and forty-five, with the same dancer's body she'd had since the eighties.

The sprawling nine-bedroom home looked exactly as Alicia remembered: three stories tall with a clay-red roof and oversize arched windows and doorways. Blooming pink bougainvillea hugged the side-terrace against a backdrop of mountains that for some reason looked older and wiser than the ones she had skied in Aspen. The entire estate shimmered in the early evening light, but that was thanks to the grids of metal scaffolding needed for the renovation. The house reminded Alicia of a beautiful alpha girl with braces—temporarily out of service with a promise to be better than ever when all was said and done.

"Forgive the jackhammers." Mariana smiled warmly, pulling Alicia into a Jovan Musk–soaked embrace as she and Nina reached the house.

"Hardly noticed," Alicia shouted, forcing a return smile. But after a nauseating, headache-inducing drive up the winding cliffside road high above the Mediterranean Sea, sandwiched between Nina and her *perro* poo–encrusted suitcases, with no AC, and Uncle's Andrea Bocelli remixes, the staccato hammering was giving her headache a migraine. The sun was setting, and jet lag was kicking in. Or maybe it was the skimpy, one–Luna Bar brunch she'd had several hours earlier. Whatever the cause, the cure certainly was *nawt* sharing a room with Nina and her graphic novels, unless the SLBR miraculously sprouted jets that showered Alicia with steaming hot lavender–infused mineral water every night before bed.

Behind her, Isobel and Celia were whispering in rapid-fire Spanish. *"Sí?"* Isobel asker her sister.

"Sí!" Celia answered, pulling her twin toward their metallic-red Alfa Romeo, which had been banished from the garage back when Fabian had bought his third Bentley. Clearly something had been decided.

"Be back soon," Celia called, slamming the door shut.

"Where are you going?" Marina shielded her kind brown eyes from the glare of the low sun. Nina crossed her arms under her boobs.

The engine grumbled to life and Isobel lowered her window, revealing the car's shiny black interior along with the blaring chorus of Justin Timberlake's "SexyBack." "Sample sale."

Marina's deep burgundy–lined lips fell to a disappointed frown. She gently placed a sympathetic deep red nail–tipped hand on her youngest daughter's shoulder.

A giant ball of hurt formed in Alicia's empty belly, like a melting snowball in reverse. Why hadn't her cousins invited *her*? Couldn't they see Nina snicker-pinching her nose as she pointed to the crusty brown clump on the left wheel of Alicia's stuffed Louis? If ever a situation called for a cousin-BFF rescue, it would be this one.

Marina opened her mouth to speak, but Isobel beat her to it.

"The samples are for A-cups only," she bellowed over Justin and the stuttering hammer.

Nina and Alicia didn't have to look at their heaving chests to understand what that meant.

"Ahhh. *Sí.*" Marina twirled a wavy strand of dark hair around her elegant pointer finger and shrugged in a well-that-answers-that sort of way.

"Lo siento," Isobel apologize-shrugged as the Alfa sped off.

"Well, now you have plenty of time to get settled," Marina said, leading the two ditched girls into the foyer.

Alicia's Miu Miu wedges echoed off the orange terra cotta floor tiles as she entered the beautiful Spansion.

Leafy green plants overflowed out of shiny copper vases like fat stomachs in tight jeans. The tall white walls were sparsely covered with framed paintings, mostly of fruit and wine bottles, and rustic wooden pews stood in various corners—possibly so elderly visitors could rest after trekking though the spacious house.

"We are adding a spa and screening room to the guest wing. So guess what that means?" Mariana didn't bother waiting for an answer. "You and Nina get to share a room this summer!" She clapped once, as if this news were more exciting than the invention of the iPhone.

Nina smirked, the sharp edges of her haircut sawing her round jawline.

"Why don't you two go ahead and catch up? I'm going to have Brunilda get dinner started."

Don't leave! Alicia wanted to scream. But her aunt was already sauntering toward the gourmet kitchen, her slender frame moving with the sexy sway of an ex–flamenco dancer still intent on working it.

"After *me.*" Nina began climbing the dark wood steps with her rough, unpedicured bare feet. *Her last name isn't* Callas *for nothing!* Alicia smiled at her own joke, then made a mental note to text the one-liner to Massie as soon as she had a minute away from the SLBR—whenever that might be.

Following Nina up the corkscrew staircase, Alicia gripped the cool iron banister before lifting her chilled hand to her throbbing forehead. But it didn't offer any relief. In reality, the real pain was two steps ahead, wagging her butt like Kim Kardashian.

Alicia's bags were already in the room when they arrived—Brunilda must have grabbed them while she and Nina were saying goodbye to the twins. One was on a fluffy ruby-red down comforter that puffed up over the copper-studded bed like a soufflé. The other was on the lumpy cot that had been covered in jewel-toned throw pillows in an attempt to hide the fact that it was a lumpy cot. Whoever delivered them had obviously been confused by the black duct tape that snaked across the azulejo-tiled floor, dividing the room into two very unequal parts. Which was totally understandable.

"What's this?" Alicia stepped into the spacious section, taking in the mountains from the elegant arching windows.

"Your new guest suite." Nina hooked a finger through Alicia's gold woven belt and index-pulled her back over the line to the tiny side. In addition to the lumpy cot, this side had a green milk crate (for her clothes?), a dust bunny collection (to keep her company?), and a black rubber-encased flashlight inside (her lamp?). The walk-in closet, red-tiled makeup vanity, sunflower yellow chaise, tapestry wall hangings, and posters of that eerily perfect ii! guy were across the border along with the comfy canopy bed. This left Alicia with a white wall and the wood bedroom door, which, when opened, slammed up against the metal frame of her "bed."

"Opposite of acceptable!" Alicia stomped her foot. "This is a veal pen."

Nina leaped on top of her duvet and folded her hands behind her head, boobs spilling out the sides of her tank top. She sighed dreamily and closed her eyes.

Alicia's heart beat ferociously against the inside of her navy shirtdress. "For one thing, my clothes have been cooped up in those bags for hours. They need to stretch and hang or they'll die from lack of circulation."

"*Escucha me*, A-*lee*-sha," Nina shot up. "This is not Westchester. You're in *my* house, in *my* country, and now we do things *my way*!"

Alicia's legs felt wobbly. She desperately wanted to collapse on her cot but somehow managed to resist. To sit would mean acceptance, and she was far from *that*.

"If you're so tough, why did you agree to pull my bags?" she fired back.

"Because Twin Sisters asked me to," Nina said, as if it should have been obvious.

"And you do everything they say?" Alicia smirked. Had she found a weakness?

"Not for long." Nina lumbered over to her vanity and bent to examine herself in the oval mirror. She finger-tossed her blond bangs left, then right. "As punishment for stealing their boots and taking them to Westchester, I had to do whatever they asked one hundred and fifty times." She turned away from the mirror and glared at Alicia, the blue kohl smudges still under her eyes. "Carrying your bags was number one hundred and forty-nine. One left and I am free."

"Hoooo-laaaa!" Celia shouted as she and Isobel barged into the room. They smelled like floral perfume and too much hair spray.

Alicia could barely look at them for fear of revealing her hurt that they'd shopped without her.

"Guess where we're going tonight?" Isobel squeezed past Alicia and strode over to Nina's side. Her slick black bun was now a bountiful mess of bed-head curls, and her lips showed signs of what was once a fresh coat of berry gloss.

"Tell them!" Celia jumped onto Alicia's cot and smile-bobbed as it squeak-settled.

"Another sample sale?" Alicia picked her dry cuticles.

"Por favor." Isobel walked over to Alicia and put her long, thin arm around her sagging shoulders. "There was no sample sale, American Cousin. That was just an excuse to keep Mother from asking too many questions about where we're actually going. We parked the Romeo a block away and snuck back to get you."

"Given." Alicia rolled her eyes, her sadness suddenly lifting like Heidi Montag's chest. "So where are we going?"

"Hotel Lindo!" the twins shouted at the same time.

"*¡Hola!* magazine is throwing a casting kick-off party for ii!, and we're going!" Celia said. She untied her chignon and finger-combed her silky black hair until it fell, covering her axlike shoulder blades. Alicia could have sworn she saw a purple streak mixed in toward the back, but didn't give it a second thought. She had Spanish celebs to impress and several outfits to sort through before they left. And that took priority.

Nina tore an article off her wall and waved it in front of Celia's face as proof. "That party is exclusive."

"*Sí*, but GR Girls get automatic VIP passes." Isobel scurried across the room on her tippy-toes and high-fived her twin. "And *we* are GR Girls."

"What's that?" Alicia asked with a playful smile in case it was something everybody knew. That way she could say "just joking" if she had to.

"Each summer Hotel Lindo hires two very beautiful, very stylish, very cool, very skinny girls to wear designer clothes, party with the guests, and make them believe that two very beautiful, very stylish, very cool, very skinny girls would want ever, in a million years, want to party with their greasy tourist butts."

"How did you get those jobs?" Nina squinted with skepticism. "They only go to top models."

Celia tugged her purple hairstreak and side-glanced at Isobel. They exchanged a giggle, then quickly sobered.

Alicia desperately wanted to be on their side of the inside joke. And hated that she was forced to watch the show from the LBR seats in the cheap section.

"And the best part is we can each bring a guest," Isobel beamed.

"Ehmagawd!" Alicia clapped and toe-bounced.

Nina punched the air like a lotto winner. "Thank you so—"

"Isobel will bring Cousin, and I will bring Ralph Lauren." Celia threw her head back and cackled at her own joke.

"Grassy!" Alicia hugged her bony but beautiful cousin.

Nina lowered her fist.

"So where is my date hiding?" Celia lifted the iron latch on the wood door of the walk in closet and quickly sifted through the hangers. "All I see are loose-fitting garments made of thin fabric." She poked her head out and knit her alluring thick black brows. "Who has seen Ralphie?"

"He's trapped in the suitcases." Alicia was happy to offer. "Fighting for his last breath."

"What?" the twins gasped.

"Your sister won't let me on the big side of the room with the closet, so I guess Ralphie will stay crumpled in my bags all summer." She paused to let the horror of the situation sink in. "Unless you think I should stuff them in this dusty crate." She kicked the plastic cube for effect.

"*Dios!*" Celia covered her mouth in shock. "I assumed the big half belonged to Cousin."

"Opposite of true." Alicia sneered at Nina.

"Switch!" Isobel clapped twice. "Ralph must hang."

"No way!" Nina stood on the duct-tape boundary and firmly placed her hands on her hips.

"You must!" Isobel marched behind Nina and pushed her to the small side.

"It's my room!" Nina stepped back over the line.

"You will do it, and it will count as number one hundred and fifty," Celia insisted.

Nina gasped. "But—"

"No discussion." Isobel tugged the Louis bags over to the closet, locked eyes with Alicia, and made an all-yours gesture with her hands.

"Cousin, let us know when you have finished unpacking so we can get dressed together. We can offer plenty of make-up and ii!'s 'The Rain in Spain' single. Preparations will take place in here. We will Cruz like Penélope in the Alfa when the sun goes down. Okay?" Celia asked.

"Given." Alicia beamed.

"Can't wait!" Nina beamed too.

"What makes you think you're going?" Isobel asked.

"These." Nina pushed open the window by her ex-bed and dangled the Alfa car keys over the man-made lake below.

"Give them back!" Celia lunged.

Nina quickly pulled them back.

"How did you get those?" Celia huffed.

"*Ahhhh.* The hand is quicker than the eye, sister." Nina grinned like a proud pickpocket.

"Fine." Celia held out her hand. "But don't talk to us in public."

"No problem." Nina dropped the keys in her sister's glistening palm. "I will stay close to Cousin the entire time."

"Good," Celia said.

Even though it sooo wasn't!

The line outside Hotel Lindo was Miley-Cyrus-on-tour long. It curved around the back of the hotel, which was shaped like giant pink marble L, and continued to grow as limo after limo pulled up to the valet parking attendants. Apparently, every SLBR with a pair of high heels and fake lashes had decided tonight would be the night they'd catch a glimpse of ii!

But they were wrong.

Anger-peering at the bouncers, wondering why they weren't moving forward, the wannabes fanned their faces and reapplied their lipstick so they'd have something to do besides anger-peer and wonder why they weren't moving forward. The crashing surf, located directly behind the hotel, seemed to echo their rage. Not that the bouncers cared. Rocking on the heels of their white leather Vans, they glanced up at the starry sky as if they were alone at a bus stop, contemplating life on a warm summer night.

"There's no way I can stand on that line in these . . . *things*." Alicia pointed to the silver open-toe boots she'd let Isobel talk her into. They *did* look *caliente* with Celia's white pony-hair miniskirt (don't tell MB), pewter chain belt, and ivory gauze halter. If the Pretty Committee had seen her *ew*-fit, they'd have put her on trial for crimes against fashion. But she had to put the *S* in Spalpha somehow, and everyone was envy-staring.

"*Por fah-vor,* American Cousin, we will not be standing on any *line,*" Celia practically spat, marching straight toward the blue-eyed bouncer with the buzzed head and bronzed arms. He stood in front of a red velvet rope, wearing a white linen suit and hugging a clipboard to his shirtless chest.

"*Hay una cola.*" He tilted his head to show them the line, just in case they'd somehow managed to overlook it.

"We're Guest Relations," Isobel insisted, purposely popping the collar on her black and white–striped blazer so he could spot the black Ralph Lauren label. Then she turned and adjusted the back of her bloodred short shorts, casually revealing the same label, proving her fabulousness wasn't restricted to her upper half.

He eagerly scanned her long, oil-slicked legs, then consulted his clipboard. "*Nombre?*"

"Celia and Isobel Callas, plus two," Celia said, like it should have been obvious.

"Ahhh, *síí.*" His eyes crinkled with kindness and his expression softened. "Forgive me. It's just that your outfits confused me." He finally spoke English.

"*Why?*" Celia jumped back as if his words were fire. "What's wrong with our *designer* outfits?" She grabbed her 100 percent silk navy wide-leg pants in one hand

and matching beaded vest in the other and squeezed the delicate fabrics in her quaking fist. "This Ralph Lauren is *hawt* couture. From Ah-merica!" The canary yellow canvas riding cap (also Ralph) atop her blowout nodded in consent.

Nina stepped forward. "And in case you were wondering, I DIY'ed these jeans!" She lifted her skinny leg and showed him her purple and blue tie-dyed denim. "They may not be in America yet, but they will be soon."

Alicia turned away, pretending she hadn't heard her cousin's embarrassing admission. Or noticed her two different-colored ballet flats—one silver and one gold—or her teeny green bikini top, which she was trying to pass off as acceptable.

"I like your outfits *veryvery* much," the bouncer said to Nina's D-cups.

"Let us in!" yelled a delusional American girl from the middle of the line.

"*Síííííí!*" shouted others.

The bouncer held up his palm, putting an immediate end to their spontaneous uprising.

Alicia felt wonderfully superior, like when she was seated in first class and got to watch all the LBRs in coach trudge to the back of the plane. Being "in" with the bouncer at Barcelona's luxe new five-star hotel—on her first night—was Spalpha times ten.

"Then what's the problem with our outfits?" Celia pushed

Nina aside and smoothed her wild hair to combat the onset of ocean-air frizz.

"It's just that Esmeralda has Versace gowns for the GR girls. They are not from America, but they are *veryvery* sexy and—"

"Versace! *Where?*" Isobel began unbuttoning her blazer.

"Inside your suite." He dug his dark hand in his white linen pant pocket and pulled out a credit card–size mirror. "This is the key. Your summer wardrobe and all necessary accessories are there for you. If you need anything, I will be *veryvery* happy to take care of you." He winked one blue eye. "Welcome to Lindo."

"ADM!" Celia and Isobel shouted at the same time. Then, as if rehearsed, they quickly applied Clinique's A Different Grape to their puffy lips and kissed the side of his stubbly face, leaving behind two purple smooch marks to show their gratitude.

Alicia side-glanced at the bouncer, hoping he'd ask what ADM meant.

"What is ADM?" He grinned nervously while petting his soiled cheek.

Yes!

"Ay Dios mío!" they giggled.

Alicia smiled triumphantly at the Spanish version of "ehmagawd." *Muy* Spalpha.

"Let's go to our suite and get changed." Celia pushed past the bouncer, no longer needing him or Ralph Lauren.

The crowd booed and hissed as the foursome entered the pink L-shaped hotel.

No one inside the open-air marble lobby was wheeling luggage, exchanging foreign currency, or studying maps with the concierge. Instead, heavily perfumed locals whisper-huddled every time a group of good-looking boys passed. They'd quickly prop their cameras, then lower them once they realized it was just another group of hot guys and not ii! and his entourage. Meanwhile, several iridescent blue peacocks strutted around like supermodels during Fashion Week. They had an air of entitlement about them, like they knew something Alicia didn't.

"Check out these elevators!" Isobel pointed at the doors, which doubled as two upright aquariums filled with pink mini dolphins, purple starfish, and dozens of luminous fish. Celia hurried over and smashed a crystal ball–size UP button that contained two live sea horses.

"Careful! You'll kill them!" squealed Nina as the sea horses swam into each other amidst an explosion of effervescent bubbles.

Celia gave her sister a shove when several onlookers gave her the evil eye for overpressing.

"Ow!" Nina pout-shouted as she rubbed her bare arm in an obvious attempt to milk more sympathy from the compassionate crowd. But they had already turned away to continue search-stalking the elusive pop star.

A faint hiss signaled that the elevator was slowly dropping down the vertical part of the L, where the guest rooms were. Alicia wished the Pretty Committee could have been there with her to see the spectacular hotel. Or rather, she wished she were on some sort of reality show and they were sitting at home watching her. That way they could distance-envy her and not make her feel like a SLBR for wearing open-toe boots, which, by the way, she was starting to ah-dore.

The aquarium doors parted and three giggling blondes wearing white mesh "ii! ♥ ii!" off-the-shoulder T-shirts scuttled out. A mix of vanilla and cigarette smoke lingered in the elevator, where a live feed of the raucous dance party by the pool was projected onto the white walls and a thumping remix of Lily Allen's "Smile" blasted in surround sound.

"Woooo-hoooo!" Isobel grabbed her twin sister's arm and yanked her inside the movable nightclub. They lifted their black cuff–covered arms above their heads and began turning their heads from side to side like they were trying to take secret sniffs of their pits. Their narrow hips gyrated, and their high heels lifted and lowered like they were on a gold, glitter-carpeted Stairmaster.

Alicia was about to step into the elevator, but Nina shoulder-shoved her out of the way, shaking her platinum-blond bowl-with-bangs haircut like it was crawling with flying beetles. Celia immediately butt-bumped her back into the lobby and jammed her bony elbow against the CLOSE button. The doors slammed shut, leaving Alicia alone with Nina for the second time that day.

Had they *meant* to shut her out? Or was it just another example of them working on some sort of master plan that would reveal itself when the time was right? Either way, Alicia was standing like an SLBR, next to an SLBR, in the lobby of the best hotel in Spain, when she should have been proving her Spalpha-ness to ii! and his entourage.

Without another thought, Alicia rolled back her spray-tanned shoulders, lifted her pert nose in the cigarette smoke–filled air, and marched her open-toe boots though the lobby to the party outside. She didn't need Celia or Isobel any more than she needed Massie. Because a true Spalpha should be able to work a party solo, even if she was in another country with a half-naked Q-Tip in mismatched ballet flats lagging a few feet behind her.

The universe obviously was testing her. And Alicia was determined to score big.

"ADM!" Alicia blurted when she stepped away from the lobby and into a party that looked like it had been masterminded by Willy Wonka.

A giant mirrored conveyor belt supported by small, black glitter–covered pillars snaked around the L-shaped pool, offering brightly colored cocktails, an assortment of tapas, gum, mints, water, perfume, cologne, candy, soda, ii! CDs, ii! caps, ii! beach balls, and special edition ii!Pod Nanos to anyone within grabbing distance. Alicia was about to grab five—one for everyone in the Pretty Committee—but stopped herself. Massie would never act that openly excited over freebies. According to *her*, alphas had three options when it came to swag:

- Act like you already have it. (Then buy it.)
- Act like you could easily get it—if and when you decided it was worth having. (Then buy it.)
- Act like it sucked and you didn't want it. (Then buy something better.)

Alicia forced herself to turn away to avoid further temptation. Instead she looked up at the dance floor, which was located on the roof of the horizontal part of the L over the main lobby, and accessible by a ski resort–style chairlift. According to two girls chatting loudly next to her, the blaring music was from a series of playlists created by ii! himself.

But the best part was that the wild affair was completely unsupervised by the hotel staff—except for the Lindo peacocks, who roamed the grounds with their luminous feathers splayed to remind the glamorous guests that they had just as much reason to be there as anyone. There were no waiters with over-bleached teeth butting into people's conversations and wagging stinky trays of food under their noses. No security teams or barrel-chested bodyguards with curly wires in their ears. Just tanned and toned VIPs who'd managed to score invites to the only event to make Westchester's fetes look like bounce-house birthday parties with Happy Meals. It was a "no parents" party on a "parents only" budget. It was the Spalpha epicenter. And Alicia was there!

While Nina hovered over the conveyor belt, filling the pockets of her tie-dyed jeans with all things ii!, Alicia slipped behind the colorful Swarovski crystal–covered statue of some bullfighter. He was waving a sparkly red blanket and puffing out his chest with courage as a shimmering brown bull charged toward him. It was the perfect place to search the crowd for the pop star without looking like a pathetic crowd-searcher. After years of hitting the party scene with Massie, Alicia had learned one very important lesson: Know the game before you play. Jumping in without a strategy was social suicide. According to the Walpha—Westchester alpha—it was the same as going to a new mall without studying the store directory.

Crouching behind the bull's butt, Alicia had to shimmy left, then right, to avoid being spotted by the passing guests, all of whom—for some weird reason—felt compelled to pull ice cubes out of their drinks and whip them at the beast's hoofs. Some even bent down and lip-kissed the matador's jeweled feet.

Suddenly, someone tapped her shoulder. Startled, Alicia whipped her silky brunette head around.

"If you want to sniff poo, you should go home to your suitcase." Nina giggle-pointed to the bull's behind, which was awfully close to Alicia's pert nose.

"What are you doing here?" Alicia asked Nina's pockets, which were overflowing with ii!Pod Nanos in every color.

Just then a fistful of ice cubes pelted the side of Nina's thigh. Nina immediately Spanish-cursed the thrower and her boyfriend in response, but instead of apologizing, the couple threw another frosty handful at Nina's DIYed legs.

"What are they doing?" Alicia quickly abandoned her hiding place to avoid getting hit by another icy round.

"It's an old tradition." Nina knelt toward the matador's feet. Two ii!Pod Nanos fell to the puddle-soaked ground. "This is Juan Belmonte," she said before kissing his crystal-covered shoes twice. "He is the most beloved matador in the history of our country." She collected her Nanos and stood. "This statue was commissioned by the hotel's owner for millions of dollars. During his birth month of May, people from all over the country come to pay their respects."

"So what's with the ice?" Alicia asked quietly, just in case ii! was lurking within earshot and overheard her asking about basic Spanish history.

Nina smacked the animal's flared nostrils. "This is Granadino, the bull that took him down. We throw ice at him to douse the hellfire that burns within his heart."

"He's still alive?" Alicia asked as a hailstorm of ice bounced off Granadino's charging front thigh.

"ADM, no!" Nina spat. "But his spirit is."

At that moment, thunder rumbled overhead, followed by the sound of rain bouncing off the tiled pool deck. But no one ran for cover. Instead they pushed past Juan Belmonte and piled onto the chairlift. Seconds later they were storming the dance floor as the unmistakable beginning of "The Rain in Spain" remix blasted from the rooftop.

"Woooo-hoooo!" everyone shouted from above as they ground and pulsed like Cuisinarts. Alicia was itching to join in and demonstrate how Body Alive's signature modern jazz moves could blend with any beat—even Broadway musical mashups. It was the fastest way to knock out the competition and fight jet lag. But she held back. The only thing worse than dancing alone would be dancing with Nina. And right now those were her only two options. Besides, it didn't look like ii! was there yet, so what was the point?

"Ho-laaaaaaaaa," bellowed Celia and Isobel as they—and a cloud of powdery perfume—attacked Alicia's senses.

Flanked by her model-tall cousins, Alicia felt like she was five years old and hiding behind the silky curtains in her parents' master bedroom again. Only this time the "curtains" were designed by Versace and made of fuchsia chiffon (Celia's) and pleated lime green tulle (Isobel's). The strappy gold sandals that peeked out from under their gowns were from Choo's resort collection. Their makeup was all shimmer and dew, and their hair had been styled with the three B's in mind: big, beachy, and bed-head. If it hadn't been for their gyrating hips, Alicia would have sworn she was looking at a glossy fashion layout in *Vogue*—the adult one.

"Look who we found in the elevator." Celia stepped back—to the beat of the song—and yanked three impeccably dressed boys into their circle. Seconds later they were throwing their heads back, laughing and dancing, while the people up top looked down and envy-stared.

Despite the silver open-toe boots, Alicia felt short and invisible. Was she awnestly wearing a mesh top while they were in *Versace*? First ditched, now duped, Alicia missed the comfort and security of the Pretty Committee more than she ever had. What was she supposed to do now? Join their mini mosh pit? *Por fah-vor!* She hadn't even been formally introduced.

Thankfully Isobel noticed Alicia's awkward, I'm-having-fun-even-though-I'm being-ignored smile and stepped in.

"Cousin, this is G, S, and P." She tapped the three sandy-haired boys on their heads. "They're triplets. Just like us, plus one."

The boys seemed high-school age, with their semi-stubbly cheeks and confident grimaces. But they were wearing khaki Hugo Boss sport coats over their jeans, so Alicia had no clue how old they really were. Not that it mattered—they were true Spalpha arm candy.

"Encantada de conocerte." Alicia smiled, giving each one a solid two seconds of extreme eye contact while she shook their strong hands. Their light brown eyes twinkled their nice-to-meet-yous, and she knew they meant it.

"These guys work for ii!," Celia explained. "P is his personal assistant, S handles his schedule, and G—"

"Gets his girls!" P and S shouted at the same time. They exchanged a boisterous round of high-fives.

"You know," Nina wiggle-jumped into their circle. "When you put 'em all together, your initials spell *pigs.*"

Everyone stopped dancing—except her.

"I'm Nina." She brushed her white-blond bangs to the side and pulled back her shoulders, acquainting them with *her* initials: double D. "I'm Celia and Isobel's younger sister."

"Only by marriage," Isobel tried.

Alicia and the boys exchanged a confused look.

"So where is ii!?" Celia asked, quickly changing the subject.

"I imagine he's in our private cabana." S pointed to the green and white–striped tent by the pool. Several girls were huddle-hovering close by, biting their nails and side-staring at the triplets, hoping their new lip glosses and high heels might earn them personal invites inside.

"Lead the way." Celia tossed her messy black hair and linked arms with G—or was it P?

Alicia, refusing to be left behind for a third time that day, made every effort to stay close to her cousins and far away from Nina.

Only, she hadn't evened managed to take three steps forward when a pale fifteen-year-old boy came between her and the twins.

"Lo siento," Alicia offered her *excuse me* in Spanish, catching a whiff of his sporty deodorant.

"'Ello," he said with a big grin that advertised his slightly crooked eyetooth. He had dark blue eyes, light blond hair, and Saltine-colored skin. A long gold chain hung down his tight tank top and swung just above the waist of his black Seven jeans. He was definitely cute in a Beckham sort of way, but didn't look Spanish at awl.

"Beg yoh pah-dun, but may I ask you—"

ADM! A Brit! Code red! Alicia had to get away from him aysap before he blew her cover. The last thing a Spalpha needed was to get trapped in an *English* conversation.

She shot him a you-must-have-me-confused-with-someone-who-speaks-your-language look and squeezed by. *"No habla Inglés. ¡Adiós, chico!"*

"But—"

Alicia barely took another two steps before she was stopped again—this time by Nina. "Get out of my way!"

Nina pulled a red ¡i!-shaped lollipop out of her back pocket and jammed it in her wide mouth. "You know they're using you, right?"

Alicia's heart started to pound. She hated when people told her things she secretly suspected, but hoped weren't true. But this couldn't be one of those times, right? Nina was obviously jealous of her relationship with the twins, and was clearly desperate to sabotage it. Maybe she was shaky because of the time difference. Or perhaps her chest was synching like an iPod to the pulsating base of the Spanish song blasting from the rooftop?

"What are you talking about?" Alicia widened her already wide brown eyes.

"They don't want to hang out with you, Cousin." Nina exhaled dramatically, shooting her cherry breath all over Alicia's face. "They want to hang out with Ralph."

Alicia strained to see through the guests, hoping the twins had stopped to wait for her while she navigated LBR patrol.

But they hadn't.

Their fuchsia and lime green Versace gowns were already distant specks in the crowd, like blotches of color in a Monet.

"Told ya," Nina said smugly, as if reading Alicia's mind.

Two peacocks crossed their path—a surreal moment that would have made Alicia and Massie crack up for days. But under the current circumstances, it was hard to summon even a light grin.

Nina smirked, clearly pleased with herself, and hooked her offensive hair behind an ear, revealing a turquoise hoop earring. The sight of it transported Alicia to last summer and the relaxing weekend she and her mother had spent boutiquing in Greece.

"Hey, wait! Those are mine." Alicia reached for the hoop.

Nina jumped back and the earring swung back, too, taunting Alicia and mocking her desperation.

Alicia's bottom lip began to quiver. But *why*? Was she hungry? Tired? Lonely? Confused? Humiliated? Yes, yes, yes, yes, and yes. But crying in public was only for funerals, where waterproof mascara was a must. Instead she summoned her inner Spalpha and reached for the earring again. This time she managed to hook her finger through it. Nina's ear stretched out like the skin on an old lady's elbow.

"Ow!" Nina shoved Alicia. *Hard!*

Alicia lost her balance in the silver open-toe boots and almost fell backward. But years of dance had trained her to catch herself before hitting the ground.

"My ear is bleeding!" Nina huffed, lifting her index finger to show off the tiny dot of blood.

Alicia strained her eyes to assess the damage. "That's not blood. It's part of your stupid lollipop."

A few people who had gathered to watch the *chica* fight snickered at Alicia's keen discovery.

"It's blood!" Nina insisted.

Alicia, now playing to the growing crowd, flicked the lollipop chunk to the ground.

More laughter.

"Now give me back my earrings before I call the police," Alicia shouted, so her fans could hear. "Just like I did last time you stole from me."

Nina lowered her head, lifted her eyes, and charged straight for Alicia, just like Granadino. Alicia jumped out of the way—just in time to see Nina slam straight into Juan Belmonte's shimmering feet.

The crowd gasped.

Hoping to save the day, Alicia hurried over and quickly separated her cousin from the teetering matador. But when she wrapped her arms around Nina, one of the mesh holes in her Spalpha shirt caught on the back of Nina's stolen turquoise earring.

"Let go!" Nina grumbled, wriggling to free herself from Alicia's grasp.

"I'm stuck!" Alicia cried.

But Nina clearly didn't believe her. She shoved Alicia. And Alicia shoved back, driven by anger that was more concentrated than the nutrients in her Lemon Zest Luna Bar. The force was enough to rip the shirt from the earring, rip the earring from Nina's ear, and send them all—shirt, earring, ear, and the rest of the two girls—crashing into Juan Belmonte . . . who was tackled to death all over again.

The music stopped.

VIPs gasped.

And the peacocks fluttered off in a panic.

The limestone patio was covered in thousands of crystals, which no one dared take or even touch. Instead, they stepped back, as if each glistening stone were a live grenade.

Everyone stared at the girls, their brightly shadowed lids heavy with disgust. Even Juan's glass eyes seemed to know who was to blame.

"It was an accident," Alicia desperately wanted to explain. But her lips felt like they were glossed with Krazy Glue, and she couldn't utter a word.

"ADM." Nina shook her head and sighed.

Suddenly the crowd parted and a very short, very stocky, rectangular-framed woman appeared before them, wearing a zipped-up white leather jacket, matching leather skinny pants, and canvas stilettos. Her frizzy black hair was tied loosely in a bun atop of her long head. The round, dime-shaped mole to the right of her lip was home to three wiry hairs, which she pulled and twisted while she surveyed the damage.

"*¿Quién es el responsable?*" She scanned the crowd with her beady dark eyes.

"*¡Ella!*" Nina stomped down on a yellow crystal and pointed at Alicia.

Everyone gasped again.

Alicia nodded in agreement, like she understood the conversation, which she didn't. But ii! was probably watching, and if she revealed herself as a clueless American tourist now, her future as a foreign video star would be opposite of successful.

"*¡Vengan a mi oficina!*" *Come to my office!* The she-dwarf gripped Alicia's ear and tugged. "*¡Ahora!*"

More than anything, Alicia wanted to threaten the little woman with a lawsuit, but she had no idea how to say that in Spanish. Instead, she gave her best Lindsay-Lohan-in-trouble-with-the-cops-again pout and silently thanked Gawd bad-girl teens were trendy.

"*Adiós,*" Nina snickered.

"*Usted también.*" The troll immediately reached for Nina's purple ear and tugged her too.

"*Soy inocente!*" Nina shouted her innocence. But the she-dwarf yanked like she knew otherwise.

After a humiliating-times-ten journey through the lobby, the girls were ear-tossed into the woman's office.

"*Siéntese.*" She chin-pointed to the two iridescent-blue, feather-covered wing chairs that faced her poured-concrete desk.

The office had a cold feel to it, even though it was nauseatingly humid and had the soggy-cereal smell of fish food. A gold plaque on the woman's otherwise empty desk took care of the introductions. It said ESMERALDA BELMONTE.

Once the girls were seated, Esmeralda slammed the door behind them. *"¡Esto es un desastre!"* she barked. Her voice was low and scratchy, like she had been swallowing Swarovskis since birth.

Alicia turned to make sure the door was shut and they were alone. Apart from an iridescent-blue peacock that was pecking insects out of a purple-lighted aquarium, they were.

"Do you speak English?" she asked sweetly. "It's not that I don't understand Spanish, it's just that—"

"She's American." Nina rolled her eyes.

"My mother's Span—"

"Enough!" Esmeralda roared. Her hair bun shook like a car teetering on the edge of a cliff. "Do you realize you destroyed the statue of my great-great-great-grandpapa Juan?"

Alicia glanced at the ESMERALDA BELMONTE nameplate on her desk. Well, that explained why she was so attached to a statue.

Esmeralda pulled a scuffed wood footstool out from under her desk and stepped on it in order to hoist herself into her tall, blue feather–covered chair. A ruby red crystal was lodged in a groove in her rubber soles, which barely hung off the edge of the seat.

The discovery would have made the Pretty Committee shake with laughter, but Alicia found it impossible to squeak out even the smallest of giggles. The twins had left her for dead, and ¡i! probably had a cabana full of "real Spanish beauties" by now. Her Spalpha days were done. D-O-N-E, done.

The hot sting of tears welled up behind her eyes again. Who was she kidding? She was too pathetic to pull off the alpha thing off at home. What had made her think she could do it abroad? Suddenly, Alicia wanted to make a "Beta Blues" playlist, hide under the covers, and cry her mascara off.

Esmeralda gripped the rough edges of the concrete-slab-turned-desk and pulled herself closer. With a grunt, she leaned forward and grabbed a wafer-size gold calculator out of a gold metal caddy. The calculator was so small it looked like it had come out of a bubble gum machine, but her baby fingers power-punched it like it was NASA-tough.

"The damage in *America* currency"—she glared at Alicia with tiny, piglike black eyes—"is twenty-nine thousand, eight hundred dollars."

Alicia breathed a sigh of relief. "Nina, you said it was worth *millions*," she whisper-hissed.

Nina shrugged, looking just as shocked.

"Do you think I am loco enough to keep the real one here?" Esmeralda slapped the metal desk with her tiny hand. The peacock in the corner pulled his long neck out of the aquarium.

"The one you destroyed is a copy." Esmeralda slid off her chair and stood. For a second, all they could see was her sloppy bun making its way around the desk. She finally appeared and faced them. "But you will still have to pay me back."

Esmeralda scuttled over to the tall stainless-steel file cabinet against the wall, opened the drawer, and pulled out two dresses, folded into stiff squares. They looked like giant dinner napkins. She tossed them on the girls' laps. "You start tomorrow."

"GR Girls?" Alicia squealed. She couldn't unfold her gown fast enough.

"Doncellas," Nina said flatly, holding up her black, boxy, knee-length polyester dress with the white *M* above the left boob. "Maids," she translated.

"More like towel girls." Esmeralda grinned, showing off a row of tiny gray teeth. "You will wash them, fold them, and fluff them. You will place them on the chairs by the pool and *re*place them when they are soiled."

Ew!

Suddenly, Alicia was very motivated to delete her Beta Blues playlist and become a Spalpha again. It was her only hope of escaping this Cinderella story.

Unless . . .

"Um, is there somewhere private I can go to use the phone?" Alicia smiled politely. "I think I can get this whole thing taken care of *immediatamente*."

"Make your call from here." Esmeralda placed her small hand on the cast-iron door handle. "Don't bother escaping. I charge roaming fees." She snort-laughed at her threat-joke, then left.

"Why is that thing staring at us?" Nina stuck out her red lollipop–stained tongue and wagged it at the peacock. Alicia ignored her as she dialed America.

"Is everything okay?" Nadia answered after the first ring.

The *bing-bong* of the Riveras' OnStar played in the background, and Alicia knew her mom was in the Lexus.

"Totally," Alicia said with a fake smile. "It's just that, well, Nina and I—but mostly Nina—kind of knocked over some stupid fake statue at a hotel and now the *ew-ner* want us to be maids to pay for it. But if you wire a check for, like, twenty-nine thousand dollars, we can all get on with our lives and—"

"*What?*" Nadia shrieked, and lowered the volume on her Jordin Sparks CD. "How much?"

Alicia cleavage started to itch. Why was her mother making such a big deal about this?

"It's twenty-nine thousand *eight hundred* dollars," Nina shouted in the background. "Not twenty-nine thousand even."

Alicia covered the mouthpiece. "Can't you even contribute a *little*?"

"It wasn't my fault!" Nina insisted.

"Ugh!" Alicia turned her back on her infuriating cousin and refocused her attention on the distress call. "So if you could just wire the—"

"Was it *your* fault?" Nadia interrupted. Alicia heard the GPS navigator instruct her mom to take the next left.

"Just a little bit, but—"

"Didn't you tell us you were responsible enough to travel on your own this summer?"

"Yeah." Alicia scoffed in a what-does-that-have-to-do-with-anything sort of way.

"Then you should be *re-spon-si-ble* for getting yourself out of trouble."

The peacock plodded across the room, vilifying Alicia with his condescending bird-glare.

Alicia rolled her eyes. "Is Dad there?"

"He's still at the office," Nadia sighed. "This lipo case is sucking the life out of him."

Pun intended?

"I'll call—"

"Don't bother," Nadia grumbled. "He hasn't picked up his phone in days."

"Can't you just overnight a check and we'll talk about it when I get home?" Alicia pleaded, her hands sweating as if they already knew the answer.

"I'm sorry, sweetheart. But you're going to have to handle this on your own. Like an adult."

"But I'm going to have to do laundry and wipe off oily chairs and—"

"I love youuu," Nadia cooed.

"Well, you have a funny way of showing it." Alicia stabbed the END button with her sharp thumbnail.

Faster than Alicia could utter, "She's dead to me," Esmeralda reentered the room.

"So?" She held out her palm. "Do you have the money?"

"Um, yeah, it's on the way." She stood. "I'll drop it off as soon as it arrives."

"Nice lie, America." She popped the stiff collar of her white leather jacket.

How did she know?

"Both of you will report for work—in your uniforms—tomorrow morning at six a.m. Your debt goes up ten dollars every minute you are late. Failure to comply means I call the police and have you arrested for vandalism." She held the door open for her newest staff members, snickering as they passed.

"How am I going to get cast in 'The Rain in Spain' now? I'm an SLBR minus fifty," Alicia whined aloud as she clicked down the marble hall in her open-toe boots. She balled up her uniform in case ii! happened to be strolling through the lobby.

"Who knows?" Nina put her and on Alicia's rounded

shoulder. "Maybe his next remix will be 'It's a Hard-Knock Life' from *Annie*. You'd be perfect for that."

Alicia rolled her eyes. She didn't feel like her poo-covered suitcase anymore. Now she felt like the Juan Belmonte statue—a broken, shattered fake.

"ADM!" Celia squealed flapping her freshly manicured nails like a baby bird in flight. "We just saw ii!!"

Alicia immediately stopped fake-drying an oily Lindo chaise and lifted her sweaty brow. She blocked the mid-morning sun with her hand but still teared up from the stinging rays that managed to penetrate her skin-visor. Esmeralda had banned the use of sunglasses for all staff members—excluding GR Girls—because they came off as "aloof and superior." Apparently, adolescent blindness was the lesser of two evils.

"Liar!" Nina pinch-dropped another Hawaiian Tropic–soaked towel into the gray canvas sack they'd been dragging around the pool deck for the last forty-five minutes. Alicia would have called in sick this morning if she'd thought anyone Spanish—or anyone above a seven-point-five—would have gone for a dip or a tan before noon. But clearly the only people sunning themselves this early had been fast asleep during last night's casting party. And thus, they were ELBRs—European LBRs—and not worth the stress.

"It's true!" Isobel scurried along behind her sister. "We saw ii!'"

Alicia had no idea how to react:

Beg for details?

Scold them for leaving her in the bull-dust last night?

Ask why they hadn't begged Esmeralda to make her a GR Girl yet?

But first things first.

"Ralph Lauren didn't offer *those* in his summer collection," Alicia noted, staring at the gold RL charms that dangled from the tops of their black string bikinis and swung above their perfect innie belly buttons.

"No, Cousin, the *RL* is for 'Resort Lindo.'" Celia twirled her chain around her deeply tanned finger.

No one back home would ever *know* that. The sooner Alicia could get her hands on one of those bikinis, the sooner she could pass it off as a limited-edition Ralph. She had to have *something* to show for this summer. And after getting publicly booted from ii!'s party, snagging an RL knockoff seemed like her best, and only, option.

"The blogs said he didn't go to the party because he was mourning the fallen statue," Nina offered, like it was the final piece of evidence needed to solve a murder case.

"Not last night," Isobel whisper-hissed while maintaining a lighthearted smile so the poolside pervs would still find her fetching. After all, that was her *job*. "N-owwww!"

"*What?*" Nina dropped the gray sack and fanned her flushed cheeks.

"Where?" Alicia pulled a tube of MAC Lipglass in Lust out of her itchy side pocket.

"On his balcony." Celia adjusted the pink carnation behind her ear. "His arm was hanging over the side like this." She let her hand fall at the wrist, as if some chivalrous gentleman were about to lead her to the ballroom dance floor. "And we *totally* saw it."

"How do you know it was his?" Alicia pressed.

"It was tanned and gorgeous and covered in diamond ii! rings." Isobel bobbed up and down in her gold snakeskin Manolo slides, looking like a mocha-colored pogo stick.

Alicia glanced around the L-shaped pool to hide the disappointment in her eyes. There was no chance ii! would ever consider her a beauty now, Spanish or otherwise. Her forehead was slick with sweat, and her feet were starting to swell from the heat. Not even the ELBRs around the pool with their sagging pink bellies and salsa-stained sarongs were giving her a second look.

Except for one.

The pasty Brit who'd gotten in her way the night before was drumming his pale thigh to the beat of whatever was playing on his blue ii!Pod Nano with one hand and waving at Alicia with the other.

She whip-turned away. He wasn't Spanish, but he *was* decent looking. And she was in a boxy poly-blend maid uniform, looking opposite of cute.

A gaggle of peacocks meandered by. They glared at Alicia and Nina, practically telling them to get back to work. But when they passed the twins, they simply fluttered their spectacular wings like some secret beautiful-people club handshake.

"We better go." Celia gripped Isobel's wrist as a bare-foot production assistant in a black T-shirt and turquoise board shorts pushed a handcart filled with stage lights and wires past the girls. "The video crew is setting up today." She tipped her gold Chanel aviators and followed the buff lackey with her almond-shaped eyes. "These are people we should definitely get to know. They'll lead us right to the source."

"Good point, sister." Isobel hooked her finger around her tiny bikini bottom and pulled it out of her butt.

The twins scurried off without another word. It was official. Alicia envy-hated them more than all the times she'd ever envy-hated Massie put together.

"Why aren't you working?"

The girls turned toward the voice, but had to look down to see where it was coming from. Esmeralda had sneaked up behind them. She was wearing a green leather miniskirt and matching blazer with the same white canvas stilettos from the night before. Despite her heat-doesn't-affect-me leather ensemble, her wrinkled forehead was beading like a Vera Wang wedding gown.

"America," she snapped her fingers. "I'm moving you inside. You are too distracted out here."

"Grassy!" Alicia beamed. Air-conditioning and a break

from worrying about being spotted by P, G, S, or ii! seemed like the perfect solution to this far-from-perfect morning.

"Oh, and I made a terrible error with your uniforms," Esmeralda said, handing them each a white iridescent Hotel Lindo bag.

Finally!

Alicia couldn't wait to get out of her itchy sack and put on something worthy of a Spalpha.

"I'm sure you will find these more flattering." Esmeralda folded her short arms across her flat chest and waited with pride while the girls tore into their bags.

"ADM." Nina pretended to barf in her mouth, a gesture Alicia would have found funny if the situation weren't so dire.

"*Ewww*-niform." Alicia winced as she held up a mustard-colored starched cotton dress. The skirt ballooned out like an umbrella, the sleeves were stiff triangles, and there was a black mop embroidered over the left breast. "I'll pay you double if I don't have to wear this."

Esmeralda ignored the comment. "You may change in the broom hut and then make your way down to the laundry room. Nina, you will deliver dirty towels, and America will wash them."

She clapped her hands twice before hobbling off to sprinkle peacock food on the grass. The plumed birds flocked to her side, and she tittered with giddy delight.

After squeezing herself into the abrasive and ugly-times-a-million dress, Alicia stomped down the concrete staircase and through a door that read EMPLOYEES ONLY. Her pert nose followed the smell of fabric softener to a room marked LAVANDERÍA.

The air inside was so humid it felt like she was breathing into a massive, detergent–soaked cotton ball, and she couldn't help wondering about the effect it would have on her wavy hair.

Looking around, she saw two giant silver machines pushed up against a wall covered in chipped yellow paint—a flash-forward to Alicia's manicure if she didn't get some "me" time soon. In the far corner a peacock was nibbling on a pile of sunscreen-stained towels.

"Shoo!" Alicia waved him away like a pesky fly, but he just fanned his feathers and continued pecking.

"Ugh!" She angrily grabbed the towels away from the bird while cursing out:

Her insensitive mother . . .

The Pretty Committee, for having fun when she wasn't . . .

The twins, for snagging GR jobs . . .

The machines, for having Spanish instructions, and . . .

Nina, for being allowed to stay by the pool, where oxygen was still available.

The minute her father won his lipo case, she was going to sue them all.

"'Ello." A familiar voice echoed off the bare walls. "Me

again," the male voice said in a singsongy accent. "Nigel's the name."

Alicia wiped her slick forehead on a gazpacho-stained towel before turning to face him. His pale chest was hidden by a tattered vintage concert tee showing two cornrowed guys named Milli Vanilli.

"What are you doing here?" she asked in English, no longer caring if he knew she was half American. Her chances of being in ii!'s video were the same as Nigel's being a judge: zero minus *diez*.

"I thought you were Spanish when we met," he tra-la-la-ed. "But I 'eard you tawkin' at the pool, and you sound American." He smiled, revealing his crooked tooth once again. "That means we can hang out."

"Wait, you thought I was Spanish?" Alicia felt renewed hope as she pushed a towel tower into one of the machines and slammed the door shut. "I heart that!"

"Yeah, you look Spanish." His blush revealed that, by his standards, looking Spanish was a good thing.

"I'm half," she admitted.

Nigel's blue eyes illuminated, like Alicia had somehow gotten behind them and flicked the on switch.

"I imagine you'll be trying out for that video contest, royt?" He pinched his tee and pulled it away from his sweaty torso.

Alicia looked at Nigel closely for the first time. She had never been attracted to the fair-complected, but he was undeniably ah-dorable.

His dark blue eyes, short-cropped blond hair, toned abs, foreign accent, zitless skin, and whiskerless chin would make him an indisputable ten in Westchester. But he was British, and Alicia was on a Spalpha mission, not a Balpha mission. And that made him an unfortunate waste of time. *Pity.*

"We'll see." Alicia shrugged, cutting the conversation off like a chunk of split ends. It was time for him to leave. Time for him to stop looking at her in that crusty maid's uniform in the humid laundry room, surrounded by other people's stains.

She had considered explaining her situation, but decided that would be too complicated for someone who was a non-crush. Especially the part about her parents not bailing her out. Even *she* was having a hard time understanding that one.

"You better go." Alicia dumped half a bottle of something blue in the machine and cranked it on.

"Got some more!" Nina shouted from the top of the concrete stairs. Alicia could hear her drop the sack with a thud and kick it. It tumbled loudly down the steps. The peacock pulled back his feathers and squawked, taking off.

Alicia and Nigel bashed into each other, trying to find cover in the tiny, square room.

"Sorry," they giggle-said at the same time. Alicia quickly hurried to grab the bag, which was now lodged in the open doorway.

"Who's this?" Nina entered, circling Nigel like a hungry lion.

"He's no one," Alicia snapped. She knew her tone was harsh, but didn't care. The sooner he left, the faster the image of her in this horrific environment would fade from his British brain.

Besides, he was sucking the Spanish out of her, and she needed every bit she had.

"I'm off then." Nigel backed out of the room. "See you around?"

Alicia untied the sack, grunt-pulling out towels and pretending she was too involved in her work to respond. When she looked up a minute later, he was gone.

"It's so much cooler by the pool." Nina smirked. Her blond bangs were plastered to her forehead, and blue kohl was smudged above her cheeks. "How 'bout I help you with this next load so you can get some air."

"Seriously?" Alicia asked with squinted eyes. Had Nina actually made a kind offer? Or was the temperature causing her to hallucinate?

"Yeah. Just fill that wash bucket in the sink with water and start dumping it in the machine. Once it's full, add the towels. I'll start folding these." Nina opened the metal door and waved away the heat from the dryer.

"Wait." Alicia paused before grabbing the tin bucket. "It seems weird to add water to a dryer."

Nina rolled her eyes. "Not when the dryer works off

boiler steam." She pulled out an armload of brittle towels. "Haven't you ever done laundry before?"

"Given," Alicia lied. The closest she'd come to doing laundry was pulling the plastic off her dry cleaning. "We just have different machines at home." She quickly filled the bucket and dumped it in the empty metal cube.

"Two more should do it," Nina said, smoothing her hand over a clean white towel.

Once she was done, Alicia pulled the heavy wet towels out of the washer and jammed them in the liquid-filled dryer. Water gushed over the top and splashed onto the concrete floor, but Nina assured her that that was completely normal.

"Now crank on the switch," she instructed.

Alicia did what she was told, suddenly finding her jail sentence less taxing now that she and her cousin were working together.

Within an instant, sparks shot out everywhere. Bluish-white lights flashed from the back of the machine like firecracker burps, and smoke began huffing out the sides.

"Ahhhhhhhhh!" they screamed, colliding with the peacock as the three of them raced for the exit.

The machine continued to rattle and hiss. It sounded like someone was trapped inside, punching and kicking against the metal door. The banging got louder, the smoke got thicker, and the sparks flew farther.

"Clear the way!" shouted a husky female voice.

The girls turned and saw Esmeralda speed-walking next to two firefighters and three peacocks. The uniformed men hurried by, carrying axes and dragging hoses, their eyes fixed on the smoking cauldron ahead. Rushing in, they swung their blades and disappeared into the light gray cloud.

When they emerged, the smoke was clearing, and the room smelled like singed hair.

The men explained something to Esmeralda in Spanish before hurrying off, shaking their heads in disbelief.

Alicia watched it all from her perch on the concrete stairs. Had her cousin purposely sabotaged her, or was she just more laundry-illiterate than she cared to admit? Alicia side-glanced at Nina, wondering how she was going to explain her way out of the situation.

"American Cousin, I told you not to add water," she huffed loud enough for Esmeralda to hear.

"What?" Alicia squealed, her heart suddenly pounding and smoking like the broken machine.

"No words!" Esmeralda pulled a tiny gold calculator out of her green leather blazer pocket and tapped away at its mini buttons. "Just numbers."

She held up the total, which was now seven hundred dollars more than it had been the previous night. "From now on, you will hang the wet towels on a clothesline and you won't go home until they are dry."

Alicia's heart stopped pounding all together. She no longer felt like her *perro* poo–covered Louis Vuitton suitcase or the broken Juan Belmonte statue.

Now she felt like the dryer—all washed up.

"¡Piensa rápido!" Nina shouted before chucking a sopping wet towel at Alicia's face.

"Uggggh!" Alicia peeled the sangria-soaked shroud off her sweaty head and whipped it into the dirty towel bin. "Why are you so opposite of alpha?" she shouted, her voice capturing the attention of every sunbather on the packed pool deck. Once they'd identified the shouter as a towel girl and not a terrorist, they sigh-shifted their way back to comfort on their green canvas–covered cots and tried their hardest to forget the brash disruption.

Nina snickered and returned to the white cotton pyramid she had been Jenga-building in the "help yourself" window of the orange adobe towel hut. With a "slip" of her elbow, Alicia knocked the pyramid to the limestone deck.

"Opposite of *lo siento*." She flip-flopped out of the hut with an armload of fresh folded towels and a smile.

After nearly a week of anger-silence, Alicia could no longer ignore Nina's attention-seeking jabs. It was one thing to overlook fake fart noises, peacock feathers floating in her ice water, and stolen earrings, but it was quite another to get publicly doused like a burning toaster. Especially when ii!'s bling-covered hand was hanging over his suite balcony for the fifth day in row. Clearly, he was assessing his options from an overhead perspective while P, G, and S staked out the deck like ground troops. The triplets frolicked in and out of their private cabana, nudging one another every time a bikini-clad guest padded by. They were obviously homing in on their favorites, even though the audition wasn't for another couple of days. It was hard to compete when stuck wearing a stiff, mustard-colored yurt that smelled like a frat-house bathroom.

Nigel was the only guy around who made Alicia feel like a contender. Despite her standoffishness in the laundry room, he'd still wink-wave every time she passed his chaise. He'd compliment her on her deepening leg tan, her caramel-colored highlights (natural, of course), and the cute way she stuffed dirty towels into the gray canvas laundry bag. If she'd been on the other side of the Atlantic, the attention would have fueled her like a triple shot latte. But here, it was like wearing bright vintage Pucci to a winter funeral—the right statement but the wrong occasion. The best she could do under Esmeralda's watchful eye was unbutton her coarse uniform to give her brick red, C-cup-hugging Ralph Lauren bikini top some much-needed exposure. And each time she leaned down to replace a towel, she let the dress slide off her shoulder a wee bit more.

Oops.

By the time she got to the green and white–striped VIP

cabana, the embroidered black mop was resting on her narrow hips, and her Westchester-white chest was buzzing with the sun's invigorating rays.

"My turn!" Celia called out from somewhere behind the billowing canvas walls.

Alicia peeked through the luffing door flaps. P—or was it G or S?—was lying on his stomach. Jewel-toned satin pillows had been stripped from the wood daybeds and placed on the grassy floor surrounding his splayed torso. Isobel stood above him squirting olive oil onto his muscular back while the others looked on. Once he was slick and slippery, Celia kicked off her orange and blue Manolo slides and jumped on.

"*¡Uno . . . dos . . . tres!*" they shout-counted while Celia teetered forward and backward, trying her hardest to balance on his greasy torso. "*Nueve . . . diez . . . once . . .*"

"Ahhhhh!" Celia's left heel slipped, and she landed butt-first on his legs.

Alicia closed the flaps and choked back a wave of betrayal-barf while P and Celia scream-laughed in pain.

After not seeing the twins all morning, she'd hoped they were finally speaking to Esmeralda about bending the rules and making her the third GR Girl. Last night, when they'd asked to borrow her favorite Ralph Lauren denim mini and tangerine short shorts, she'd pleaded with them to use their GR influence to rescue her from towel-torture. But it was nauseatingly obvious that they had other priorities.

"Whose boobie shadow is on the wall?" one of the entourage boys asked.

Everyone inside burst out laughing. Before Alicia could step away and cover her cleavage, Celia appeared. Her bright, red-stained lips curled up with a mix of relief and frustration. "What are you doing here?" she whispered, closing the flaps behind her.

Alicia, over being stung by her queen-bee cousins, decided it was time to speak her mind. "I'm dropping off towels because no one offered *me* a GR position yet." She stood firm, studying her reflection in Celia's mirrored gold aviators, fully hearting her squinty I-mean-business glare.

"Are those diamond hoops the real deal?" Celia gently finger-flicked one of Alicia's earrings.

"Given." Alicia gazed up at ii!'s balcony, hoping his dangling hand was still there and praying he was watching her being admired by a GR Girl.

"Can I borrow them tonight?" Celia quickly checked over her shoulder, probably hoping the entourage wasn't listening so she could pass them off as her own.

"Boobie shadow!" one of them called while everyone else laughed.

Alicia felt the tremble of angry words marching toward her mouth. How dare Celia treat her with such blatant disregard? Who did she think—

"Unless, of course, *you* were planning on wearing them."

Celia twirled her finger around the gold RL chain that dangled off her black bikini and swung in her cleavage.

"Where? To bed?" Alicia snapped.

"No, with us, silly." Celia put her arm around Alicia's burning shoulders, her fingers brushing up against the diamond earrings once again.

Accident?

"We're going to Danzatoria." She threw her hands over her head and danced as if she were listening to an iPod under her yellow chiffon headscarf. "P, G, and S are picking us up at the house at eight p.m.—in a *limo.*"

"Will ii! be there?"

"You tell me." Celia knit her brows in confusion.

Alicia knit hers back. How was *she* supposed to know if . . . ohhhhhh.

"*Noooo*, I mean, will ii! the singer be there? Not ii! as in *I.*" She pointed at herself.

"Oohhhh." Celia started laughing, and Alicia couldn't help but join in. Just as they were slowing down to catch their breath, a passing peacock got them going all over again.

It wasn't long before several sunbathers were looking at Alicia for the second time that morning. Only now they probably wanted to know what the two bikini-clad hawties were laughing about. And of course how they got so hawt.

"Get dressed!" Esmeralda snapped.

Alicia whirled around, coming face-to-air with the miniature manager. *Where did she come from?*

Celia kept the smile on her face, knowing full well the hotelier couldn't possibly be talking to *her*. She was right.

Esmeralda waved a wrinkled, hooked finger at Alicia's sunburned chest. *"¡Vamos!"*

Without a word, Alicia lifted her dress and buttoned it back up. It just so happened to match the mustard-colored leather vest Esmeralda was wearing over her ill-fitting white shift. It was ten kinds of wrong.

"Now back to work!" She stomped her black platform wedge sandal against the dark limestone deck.

"See you at eight," Celia said to Alicia's earrings, then hurried back inside the raucous cabana.

A blast of up-tempo salsa music spilled through the pool loudspeakers. *Had it been there all along?* Alicia moved to the thumping beat, grabbing towels, practicing her Spalpha smile, and workshopping outfit ideas in her mind. Her days of mesh tops and open-toed boots were over. Tonight she would show ii!, P, G, and S what a real Spanish beauty with *real* taste looked like. Tonight was going to be all Ralph.

While Alicia zigzagged through the west-facing rows of green canvas chairs, offering fresh towels, Nina slithered up beside her. "Spritz?" she asked, positioning a can of Evian face mist in a pruning woman's visage. The woman waved her away like an encephalitis-carrying mosquito. Happily, Nina moved on.

"Where is Celia taking your clothes tonight?" she asked Alicia through a fake-frozen smile.

"She is taking *me* to Danzatoria with ii! and the entourage." It felt so good saying it out loud.

"That place is good times." Nina giggle-sprayed a sleeping man's chiseled chest and quickly turned away when he opened his eyes.

The secret spritz reminded Alicia of something Massie might have done and she found herself giggling along with her cousin. Was it possible that she was actually starting to warm to Nina's sense of humor?

"If you want to leave early to get ready, I'll cover for you," Nina offered, spritzing a little Evian on her tongue.

Alicia froze. Was Nina actually being . . . *nice?*

"Seriously." Nina stuffed the spray can in the deep pocket of her dress.

"Quítate de en medio." A supermodel type with deeply oiled skin and long arms lazily waved Nina away.

"Oops," Nina giggled, stepping aside and removing her shadow from the woman's lithe frame. The rich golden light returned, and the woman lowered her arm.

"I mean it." Nina pulled her cousin off the crowded deck and onto the grass so they could converse freely. "I'm tired of fighting. And I already got you back for embarrassing me at your OCD school."

"And you don't want *anything* from me?" Alicia cocked her head in disbelief, silently cursing the no-sunglasses rule.

"Well, maybe one thing." Nina grinned.

Shocker!

"What?" Alicia rolled her eyes. But if it meant she could leave early, it was worth a listen.

"Esmeralda asked me to turn on the power generator in fifteen minutes, and I kind of wanted to sneak off and watch my favorite soap opera in room 718. The lock is broken and it's just sitting there wide open. So if you do that for me, I'll—"

"ADM, grassy!" Alicia grabbed Nina's clammy hand and shook it hard. "Done!"

"Excellent!" Nina shook back. "All you have to do is push the red button on the side of that metal machine over there." She pointed to the shiny cylinder by the poolside snack bar. "Just don't forget or she'll kill me."

"No prob." Alicia tapped the face of her bronze Marc Jacobs cuff-watch to show she was on top of it.

Exactly fifteen minutes later, Alicia marched over to the generator and searched for the red button. She found it without a problem and pressed it extra hard.

Done, done, and done!

The machine hummed to life. Then it rattled. Then shook. Seconds later, six nozzles rose out of the top and began spinning . . . faster and faster and faster. A massive retching sound, like the kind you make before puking, erupted from its bowels. Seconds later, water began spraying from the nozzles.

"Ahhhhhhhh!" screamed the diners who had been enjoying their late lunches under a cloudless sky. The clank of cutlery and the screech of chairs drowned out the festive music. French fries floated in water-filled baskets, and now-see-through resort wear stuck to fleeing guests.

"Tsunami!" someone shouted from the chaise area.

"Hurricane!" others cried.

Holding towels over their heads, everyone gathered their *Hola!* magazines, stuffed them in their designer totes, and scrambled for the lobby.

Alicia stood and watched in shock, barely noticing the cold water cascading over her as the porous maid's uniform instantly absorbed it.

From across the deck, Nigel threw her a supportive thumbs-up as he laugh-scrambled to safety with his two pasty mates. The only people not running for cover were the twins and triplets, who were still inside the cabana—probably covered in enough oil to wick away any water that happened to touch them. High above their heads, ii!'s hand still dangled over the suite's balcony, his chiseled abs probably quaking with laughter.

And then, the downpour stopped as suddenly as it had started.

Esmeralda and a gaggle of soggy peacocks appeared by Alicia's side. The tiny lady began shouting some mighty big words in Spanish. All Alicia understood was that she was in major trouble.

"It wasn't my fault," she pleaded. "Nina asked me to—"

"Enough!" Esmeralda placed her pruning hand in front of Alicia's face. "I saw *you* press that button, not Nina!"

"Thank you, Esmeralda, for not listening to my lying cousin," Nina said, crashing their conversation on the deserted pool deck. She stuck out her tongue and playfully caught a drop of water as it dripped off the tip of her pointy nose. "I wasn't even here when this scary storm happened."

"Yeah, but tell her why." Alicia's chest pounded.

Nina just puckered her lips. When it became clear she wasn't going to confess, Alicia looked at Esmeralda and blurted, "She was in room 718, watching soap operas."

"Really?" Esmeralda tightened her sloping hair bun.

"Yup." Alicia smirked.

"Because this hotel only has six floors," Esmeralda snapped. "Do your homework, America! You just activated the rain machine for ii!'s 'Rain in Spain' video shoot."

Nina snickered into her palms.

If Alicia had had any idea how to punch someone, Nina would have been on her way to the plastic surgeon. She'd never felt so full of rage in her entire life. She had no idea who to sue first.

"Since we have no dryer, you will stay here and blow on every one of these canvas chairs until they are crispy-dry," Esmeralda ordered.

"But I have to be somewhere at eight," Alicia heard herself whine.

"Unless it's a giant hair-dryer factory, you better cancel." Esmeralda blew a kiss to her glistening peacocks and burst out laughing. The birds fanned their feathers in approval and followed her across the puddle-filled grass toward the lobby.

Once she was gone, Alicia sniffled, put her hands on her soaked hips, and faced her cousin. "I thought you already got me back for embarrassing you at OCD."

"I did." Nina winked. "This was for calling the cops."

The next morning Alicia slammed her fist against the elevator button. The two sea horses spun and collided in a torrent of bubbles. Not that she cared. Why should *her* life be the only one spinning out of control?

"Why so angry?" Nina asked, her voice dripping with faux sweetness.

Alicia was tempted to cry-scream at her well-rested cousin about how evil her prank had been. Or how badly she'd wanted to go to Danzatoria. Or how chilly and lonely it had gotten last night once the sun had set on the wet deck. Or how pathetic she'd felt waving soggy magazines over the drenched canvas chaises while freshly showered guests dined and danced all around her.

But explaining it would have been impossible, and strangling Nina wasn't an option. After six hours of overtime Alicia's jaw was stiff from blowing on the chairs and her wrists were sore from fanning them. All she could do was pretend Nina wasn't beside her, waiting to share the elevator down to the towel room so they could waste another beautiful summer day patting down the rich and oily.

Despite the early hour on a Saturday morning, the lobby

was teeming with tittering teens hoping to get spotted by ii! before tomorrow's video auditions. They were probably hoping he'd see them and become so captivated by their beauty he'd whisk them to the front of the line. Alicia knew. She used to think that way too. Before she was in debt. Before her parents cut her off. Before the twins became GR Girls without her. Before she had an uneven tan. Back when she had hope.

The elevator dinged and the aquarium doors slid open. "Don't Stop the Music" by Rihanna was blasting at top volume. So were the twins. "Woooo-hoooooooooo!" They shout-danced their way into the lobby.

Pleated gold lamé wrap minidresses barely covered their GR bikinis. And from the confident smiles on their made-up faces, they wouldn't have had it any other way. Their black hair was teased to triple its regular volume, while the pieces around their faces were slicked and pinned to the sides of their heads. Strappy turquoise heels gave them three extra inches of height they didn't need, making Alicia feel even smaller than she already did.

As if Nina and Alicia were two insignificant guests who'd won their rooms on some tacky game show, the twins breezed by without a single word.

"Are you guys mad at me for bailing last night?" Alicia tried. They stopped, acting as if they'd just noticed her.

"You bailed?" Isobel asked, adjusting the butterfly back on her black-pearl drop earring.

"Um, yeah," Alicia said, eyeing Celia, wondering if she'd even bothered to mention Alicia was invited. "I was supposed to go out with you guys, but I had to work late so I—"

"Do you think I could borrow your yellow slip dress tonight?" Isobel interrupted. "You know, since you'll be working late again?"

"*I* was going to ask about that dress," Celia whined.

Behind them, the elevator doors dinged and kissed shut.

"I'm not working late tonight," Alicia corrected her. "Where's everyone going? Will ii! be there? Did you see him last night?"

"He got stuck at another party." Celia rolled her eyes. "Some boring industry event. But G, P, and S *promise* he'll be joining us tonight at dinner."

"What time?" Alicia asked, contemplating the yellow slip dress for herself.

"Early," Isobel blurted. "Before you get off work." She spotted G, P, and S heading into the restaurant for the breakfast buffet and grabbed her sister's arm. "Don't worry, I'll take great care of the dress."

"If *you* get the dress, I get the purple backless camisole," Celia demanded, as if it belonged to Isobel.

Before Alicia had a chance to remind them exactly whose clothes they were arguing over, they *click-clacked* away like two runway models racing to make their curtain call.

Nina leaned forward and re-pressed the elevator button. She sighed and mumbled something in Spanish.

"*What?*" Alicia asked angrily, accidentally breaking her lifetime vow of Nina-silence.

"I told you so." Nina smoothed her stiff maid's dress with a cocky stroke of her hand.

"You told me *what*?"

"I told you they were using you for your Ralphs."

Unable to hold back the tears for one more second, Alicia turned on her white flip-flop and raced to the nearest bathroom as if she were starring in an Imodium commercial.

After a solid twenty-minute stall-sob, Alicia returned to the lobby feeling like she'd just stepped off the plane all over again. Her limbs ached and her eyes burned. Only this time, instead of her heart feeling helium-light with excitement for all the things to come, it felt like a rock—heavy and hard and kicked around. Her Spalpha days were over before they had even begun.

As she ambled through the lobby-crowd in a slow, dreamlike state, a beam of light flashed before her eyes. She blinked it away, irritated by the intrusion. But it came back. Over and over again. At first she had dismissed it as a ray of sunshine until she realized the windows had been tinted in preparation for the video shoot. Perhaps it was someone's finger-bling or a kid's toy or a . . .

But none of those things could have created the blinding glare that seemed to be affecting only her. And then it dawned on her. Maybe it was a sign from the Spalpha gods.

A message to stay strong. To find her inner light. To *blind* the world with her charm and beauty.

Yes! That was it!

The more Alicia thought about it, the more she knew she was right. Alphas like Massie, the twins, and ii! weren't *born*, they were *built*. They had to fight for what they wanted out of life. The best outfits, perfect bodies, A-list party invites, or glam jobs. It was all work. And the more they worked, the more they got.

Determined, Alicia set off for the elevator with renewed strength, ready to show these Spalphas that there was more to this señorita than folding towels.

The light got bigger and brighter with each step Alicia took toward it. It was calling her, guiding her, blinding her—was this that famous bright light people saw before they died? She stepped closer and closer until it actually obstructed her vision, and she walked directly into—

"Looking for this?" Nina held up a mirrored room key, a proud, goofy grin on her face.

"Huh?" Alicia accidentally blurted. Her lifetime vow of Nina-silence was not going well.

"The light," Nina snickered. "It was coming from me. I was doing it." She tilted the reflective key back and forth in front of Alicia's bloodshot eyes as proof. Sure enough, another beam of light flashed in front of her face.

"I found it while I was cleaning out the VIP cabana."

"Whose is it?" Alicia asked, her tone intentionally frosty and blasé.

"Yours. Consider it a peace offering." Nina rolled her eyes when she realized her gesture required further explanation. "It's ii!'s room key. And I just heard he needs some fresh towels." She winked.

Alicia grimaced in an I'm-not-falling-for-*that*-again sort of way.

"I swear." Nina offered her pinky, something Alicia had taught her last summer. "I'll even go with you."

Alicia stepped aside to let a man wheeling a digital sound-board pass. They were setting up for the music-video audition, which was a mere twenty-five hours away. And the only contact Alicia had made with the pop star was with his stolen key card. "Why do you want to be friends all of a sudden?"

"What do you mean *all of a sudden*?" Nina asked, scratching her left boob with the rectangular mirror. "I wanted to be your friend when I got to Westchester. But you chose boys and the Pretty Committees over me. Now you come here and all you want to do is hang with my terrible sisters. You never liked *me*."

"Opposite of true!" Alicia stomped her flip-flopped foot. "You came to my town and stole our crushes and our clothes and now—"

"And now I stole ii!'s room key." Nina waved it in front of Alicia's face again. Then she leaned forward and whispered, "If we can get up there and find out more about him, then maybe we have a chance. . . ."

Alicia's heart began agree-thumping.

"How do I know this isn't a trap?"

Nina reached into her deep uniform pocket. "Here." She dropped two tubes of Glossip Girl—Red Velvet Cupcake and Glow-in-the-Dark Blackberry—in Alicia's hand.

"ADM! These are Massie's favorite flavors." Alicia gasped. "They went missing right after the Valentine's Day Dance." She locked eyes with her slippery cousin. "How did you get these?"

"All that matters is that I am giving them to you now"—Nina closed Alicia's fist around the half-empty tubes—"as proof that you can trust me."

"How are *these* proof?"

"I love those flavors," Nina insisted. "And if I'm lying, you can give them back to Massie."

It was totally twisted logic, but looking into her cousin's wide eyes, Alicia sensed her sincerity. Plus, she was holding a sweat-soaked towel and wearing a barf-yellow shirtdress. The only thing left to lose was her rightful place in the video. At this point, everything else was gone.

With an armload of fresh towels and the mirrored card between her Red Velvet Cupcake–glossed lips, Nina knuckle-knocked on the door to ii!'s suite. "Room service."

When no one answered, she slid the key in the slot and popped open the door.

"ADM!" the girls said at the same time. The floor and walls were made of a single, giant LED screen. Images of Hawaiian waterfalls dissolved into lush rain forests, which dissolved into dark scenes from outer space.

"I feel like I'm in a screen saver," Alicia gushed.

The picture changed again, this time to a giant grassy

field with a massive rainbow that arced over the foot of the double king bed.

"Hurry," Nina snapped. Like a true professional, she was already rifling through the bright-green bedside table drawer. She pulled out a chunky gold necklace with a giant diamond encrusted *I*. "I wonder what this is worth?"

"Leave it!" Alicia smiled, suddenly finding her cousin's illegal habit somewhat charming.

Photos of the genetically perfect *ii!* posing with an array of different but equally stunning brunettes were displayed in mirrored frames on the marble mantel above the gas fireplace. "At least we know he doesn't like blondes." Alicia smiled. "That's good."

Then she felt a regret-jolt behind her abs. "Sorry," she said to Nina's white-blond hair. "I didn't mean—"

"Por fah-vor." Nina butt-slammed the drawer shut. "Do you seriously think I like this?" She hate-tugged her bangs.

The life-size screen saver suddenly transitioned from a sunny day to a raging thunderstorm. Alicia shrugged.

"My evil twin sisters made me do this."

"Why?" Alicia asked with wide brown eyes. "How?"

"Because the cute waiter at our favorite café smiled at *me* and not them. So they made me chop off my long dark hair. The color was task number one hundred seventeen, and the cut was number one hundred eighteen."

"ADM," Alicia sighed, feeling an odd tug of sympathy for

her cousin. "Maybe if we dye it back, you'll have a better chance of getting in the video."

"I have to keep it like this until it grows out. That was task number one hundred nineteen." Nina pouted as she yanked open the cinnamon heart–covered closet door. "*Dios,* who decorated this place?"

Ay-ahhhhhh, ay-ahhhhhh, ay-ahhhhhh!

A peacock dressed in an "ii! ♥ ii!" concert tee bolted out of the closet and let out a high-pitched scream. He ran in tight circles around the room and began opening and closing his feathers at high speed, like a sugar-filled kid playing with a paper fan.

"Ahhhhhhhh!" Nina and Alicia jumped onto the massive bed and giggle-hugged each other for protection.

Nina picked a creepy hand-shaped rubber jewelry holder off one of the bed's pillows and whipped it at the frenzied bird. She nailed it on the side of its tiny blue teardrop-shaped face and knocked it straight into a video puddle. Its feathers twitched one last time, and then it was still.

It was sad, but not quite as sad as Nina's hair.

"I can*nawt* believe they made you do that," Alicia said, picking the conversation back up where they'd left it, before the peacock invasion. She jumped off the bed, leaving black Havaiana footprints all over the orange ii!-patterned special-edition silk spread.

"You thought I did this by *choice*?"

A genuine smile appeared on Alicia's face, and they both burst out laughing.

"They knew about this video audition months before it was announced." Nina pulled the silk spread off the bed and draped it over the fallen peacock. "They just didn't want me to get the part."

"Well, I say if you can't get it, *they* can't get it, either," Alicia said, suddenly feeling very aligned with her misunderstood, mis-dyed cousin. "And tomorrow, I will wear my gold Ralph Lauren mini, and you can wear my favorite Ralph headscarf!"

"I like your style—"

"AMERICA!" Esmeralda kicked open the door and raced over to the limp, silk-covered peacock. Tears rolled down her wrinkled, leathery cheeks, trickling in and out of the crevices like streams rolling over cracked rocks.

"You will pay for this," Esmeralda whimpered, checking the bird's neck for a pulse.

"Given," Alicia moaned under her breath.

Nina snickered.

Esmeralda tossed the rubber hand aside and stroked the lifeless bird's feathers. "Meet me at the peacock pen tomorrow morning at ten." She grasped his little orange claw in her hand.

Ay-ahhhhhh, ay-ahhhhhh, ay-ahhhhhh!

All of a sudden, the peacock sprang back to life, screeching as loudly as his injured head could bear.

Esmeralda held him close until he stopped.

"How about noon instead?" Alicia pressed, now that the creature was safe.

"Why?" Esmeralda examined the stained bedspread and began punching numbers into her gold calculator. "Did you actually think I'd allow you to audition after the trouble you have caused?"

"But—"

"Failure to be at the peacock pen by ten a.m. will result in prompt dismissal, and I doubt you can pay your tab without this job."

She marched out, carrying the weak peacock in her tiny arms.

The image on the LED screen changed to a live shot of the hotel entrance, where a long line of beautiful girls was already starting to form for tomorrow's audition. And one of them would be taking *her* place.

Now Alicia felt like ii!'s bedspread—a thing of beauty that had been walked all over and left for dead.

PERDIDO
Una cadena muy caro.
Por favor, regresar cadena a °i! ante que llame
a la policİa.

Alicia didn't completely understand what the handwritten LOST sign in the elevator meant, but she tore it down anyway and crumple-stuffed it in her pink, shell-covered clutch. The words *lost, necklace,* and *police* were enough of a tip-off. Nina had obviously stolen ii!'s neck-bling when they were in his suite earlier that afternoon, and he was prepared to press charges. Turning her in was something to consider. Maybe then she'd finally stop stealing. But Alicia couldn't stand to lose her. Not today. Nina had a plan to take the twins down, and *that* was a major priority.

They'd promised to meet in the rooftop lounge at 5 p.m. Because, according to Nina, *everyone* would be there, and she wanted the twins to be embarrassed by as many people as possible. Alicia could hardly wait.

Esmeralda had forbidden the towel girls to attend the weekly PS (post-siesta) party, but the troll had taken the fallen peacock to the vet and wasn't expected back for at least another hour. There had been just enough time to buy a tacky vinyl bag, trendy open-toe sand-colored boots, and a royal purple shift dress from the Lindo boutique, followed by a quick drive-by of the roof. According to Nina, that was all it would take.

"I see why they call it happy hour," Alicia said, when she met up with Nina at yet another mirrored conveyor belt. It snaked around the sunny, grass-covered rooftop, offering free tapas to the bikini-buff guests who were elbow-to-elbow, admiring the sea view while secretly admiring each other.

"Year 3000" by the Jonas Brothers had everyone dancing, spilling their drinks, and laughing about it. But no one seemed to be having more fun than the twins. They were bobbing to the beat on G and P's shoulders while S sprayed them with Pellegrino. The other guests sneaked side-glimpses of them, partly wishing they were having as much fun, but mostly hoping they'd fall.

"Did you see *this*?" Alicia whispered. She opened her clutch, revealing the crumpled sign.

Nina grinned. "Isn't it great?" Her hazel eyes widened, revealing gold flecks that matched the maid uniform she still had on. "I made them during my 3:15 bathroom break."

"*You* made these?" Alicia whisper-shouted.

Nina bit her bottom lip and nodded coyly.

"So you *didn't* steal the necklace?" Alicia took a yellow plate of scallop ceviche off the belt in an effort to look less shocked.

"No, I *did*."

"*What?*"

Just then a thin man wearing a green Speedo and a white linen blazer came dangerously close to dance-bashing them into the conveyor belt.

"*Lo siento,*" he muttered, then shimmied back to a girl in a black Versace one-piece holding an umbrella drink the size of her gold bangle–covered arm.

"Maybe we should get this over with before we break something else." Alicia stepped aside just to be safe. "What's your big plan? What do I have to do?"

"*Mire y aprende,* Cousin. *Watch. And. Learn.*"

Nina began shoving her way through the crowd, and Alicia followed her. It was the opposite of Spalpha to go along with someone else's revenge plot, but it was hard for her to think like a leader while she was wearing a bile-colored polyester dress with an embroidered mop above the boob. Maybe once the twins were out of the picture she'd be less distracted and would have more time to think of ways to—

"'Ello again." Nigel appeared before Alicia and shoved a fizzing glass of limeade under her chin. "A limey from a Limey." He chuckled. "Lovely to see you up and about and not stuck in that dreadful—" He stopped himself. "I mean, it's good to see you."

Nina was waiting impatiently behind him, crossing her eyes and sticking her tongue out at the back of his blond head. But still, Alicia felt compelled to clear something up.

"I'm nawt poor, you know," she told his navy blue eyes. He blinked several times, as if his lids were trying to explain the things his lips couldn't seem to articulate.

"Never said you were." He tittered nervously.

"I'm *rich*." She took the limeade and helped herself to a long, entitled swig. "I'm only doing this towel girl thing because I half-broke the Juan Belmonte statue *andsomeotherthings*, and my parents are trying to teach me a lesson. *Which*, by the way, I refuse to learn."

A light breeze blew Nigel's unbuttoned denim shirt wide open like he was in some sort of boy-band video, revealing his slightly tanned chest. It was a definite improvement but still a blatant reminder that he was British. And peacock duty be damned, Alicia was determined to find a way to audition tomorrow. And when she did, the last thing she needed was a melatonin-deprived bloke cheering her on from the sidelines, reminding everyone that English was *not* her second language.

"*¡Vamos!*" Nina clapped twice like a saucy flamenco dancer.

"I better go." Alicia tried to squeeze past him.

"Why are you always running away from me?" he shouted just as the song was changing. Everyone turned to see who the desperate guy with the accent was pleading with.

Thankfully, "Low" by Flo Rida began blaring, and everyone turned away, hoping to get an upgrade on their dance partners.

"Gawd, will you puh-lease stop talking English!" she whisper-hissed. "I don't need everyone knowing I'm Fannish. What if ¡¡! can hear you? Then I won't qualify for the video and—"

"Fannish?" He crinkled his light eyebrows and half-smiled in anticipation.

"Fake Spanish."

"So that's what this is all about? A stupid video shoot?"

"¡Va-MOS!" Nina pointed to an invisible watch on her wrist.

"It's not *stupid*," Alicia pouted, suddenly feeling very . . . stupid. "In Westchester everyone's all American-ish, and here everyone's all Spain-ish, and I'm not all anything. I'm a mutt."

"What's wrong with being both?" Nigel lowered his eyes, like he was asking himself just as much as he was asking her.

"*Both* means I don't know what box to check when I'm filling out a skin survey at the makeup counter. It means I don't belong anywhere."

"Maybe it means you're lucky enough to belong in two places."

"Whatevs." Alicia rolled her moist eyes. This was starting to feel a little too Dr. Phil for a summer afternoon in

Spain. "Grassy for the drink, but I have to go." Even though the Fannish part of her wanted to stay, Nigel couldn't do anything to further her Spalpha status. And, like a beautiful pair of Jimmy Choo heels that were too high to walk in, she would simply have to settle for something more useful.

"*Por fah-vor,* let's go!"

Suddenly, Alicia was being wrist-pulled through the crowd and away from Nigel's sad blue eyes.

The twins were still bobbing when Nina stopped behind them. "Follow my lead." She brushed by Celia, who had a red Fendi feather clutch swaying from the crook of her elbow.

In one fluid motion, Nina opened her palm and dropped ii!'s glittering necklace inside.

"ADM!" Alicia mouthed once they passed.

"Framing is an art intended for more than just pictures, Cousin."

"Point!" Alicia lifted her finger and smiled.

"Now watch this." Nina opened Alicia's shell-covered purse and pulled out the crumpled sign. She made her rounds, showing the photo of the necklace to as many guests as possible. And then she picked her mark.

"Him." She pointed at a pregnant-looking man with a glass of sangria in each hand and the kind of wobble reserved for those walking on an airplane during turbulence.

"Uno . . . dos . . ." On *tres,* Nina shoved him straight into Celia and G—or was it P?

"ADM!" Celia called, as she swayed left, then right. She managed to steady herself on Isobel's narrow shoulders, but her bag crashed to the ground and spilled open.

"Perfecto!" Nina clapped as she and Alicia quickly backed away from the scene of the crime.

"Perfecto times ten!" Alicia high-fived her cousin. Delete the whole thieving thing and the blond Dora bob, and her cousin would have definite Spalpha potential.

"Is that ii!'s missing necklace?" Nina began whispering in various people's ears. Finally, a long-haired sleepy-eyed blonde in a black knit cap and a blue and orange tie-dyed bikini pointed at the shimmering clump. She began shouting something in Spanish. Whatever she said was enough to make the music stop. A crowd gathered around the twins.

Alicia and Nina stood on the edge of the commotion and watched with nail-biting enthusiasm.

S bent to receive the necklace before lifting the precious pendant to his full lips and kissing it. Hard. *"¡Celia, ya lo he encontrado! ¡Ya lo he encontrado!"*

"Yes!" Alicia turned to Nina, ready to rejoice. But her cousin's bug eyes and slack jaw told her to hold off on celebrating just yet.

"Ya lo ha encontrado," Nina sighed. "They think she *found* it!"

The entourage surrounded Celia and enveloped her in a massive relief-hug, like she was a child who'd gone missing at Disney World.

It was difficult to understand what Celia was saying amid the celebratory double-cheek kisses, but it was clear from her proud smile that she was taking full credit for the bling retrieval.

"Looks like someone just scored a spot in the video," a bitter redhead in a white string bikini and mirrored Diors told her sunburned BFF.

"You're right about that." Sunburn squinted at ii!'s balcony. His hand was still hanging over the railing, but this time he was making a thumbs-up sign. He must have seen the whole thing.

Alicia sighed. "How did Celia pull that off?"

"I've been asking myself that same question for the last thirteen years." Nina crumpled up her sign and threw it on the ground.

The familiar thunderclap that kicked off ii!'s "Rain in Spain" remix distracted everyone from the mini jewelry drama and revved up the party once more. But for Alicia, it was a bitter reminder that the audition was only one day away and she was doomed to watch from the peacock pen.

And then the song's rain sounds came. *Plinkkkk. Pluunck. The rain in Spain stays mainly on the plain! Plinkkkk. Plinkkkk. Pluunck. Plinkkkk. Pluunck.*

At first they song's chorus reminded her of the terrible night she'd spent hand-fanning the sopping deck. Then came the image of everyone scream-shouting their way to the lobby. And that image sparked an idea, which, if executed properly, could keep the twins from the audition. And earn *her* a spot in the Spalpha hall of fame.

Boo-woop. Boo-woop. Boo-woop.

Even Spanish alarm clocks had accents.

Alicia slapped her palm against the OFF button and cracked open the thin can of Red Bull she had chilled in a silver champagne cooler by her bed. After a long swig and dainty burp, she padded over to Nina's half of the room to nudge her awake.

"Drink." Alicia offered her the frosty can.

"Grassy," grumbled her cousin before sitting up and guzzling the cherry medicine–flavored energy drink.

Alicia sat on the edge of Nina's lumpy cot. The rusty coils cried out loudly in pain, and she quickly jumped up.

"Don't worry, the twins sleep with a sound machine in their room. They can't hear a thing." Nina tossed the empty silver can on her floor and bounded out of bed like a superhero ready for battle. "Let's do this!"

"What do you want? Roof or room?" Alicia pulled out a gold fifty-cent euro.

"Room," Nina blurted, stating the obvious choice. "Heads."

Alicia thumb-tossed the coin, caught it, and slapped it on the back of her hand with *muy* Spalpha attitude. She lifted her hand and sighed with relief. "Tails. Roof."

"ADM." Nina sighed, then crossed her chest in prayer.

Quickly, while Alicia hummed the theme song to *Mission: Impossible*, the girls changed into black-on-black sweats. They smudged Kimora Lee Simmons's Noir eye shadow on their faces and stuffed Nina's Day-Glo hair in the shower cap Alicia had colored with a black Sharpie. She looked like a giant blush brush.

"Be safe." Alicia grabbed the CD she'd burned after work and crept toward the hall.

"Ten cuidado," Nina whispered back, then hurried outside to the garden shed.

Alicia stood outside the red sliding barn door to the twins' suite, her ear pressed against the wood. The only things that seized her senses were the smell of lavender bathwater and the muffled crash of waves beating against the virtual shore of their soothing sleep machine. Other than that, all was still.

Slowly and cautiously, Alicia slid open the door. She tiptoed inside. A long corridor dimly lit by a cast-iron candelabrum guided her to the twins' sleeping chamber.

The semicircular room was shaped like a giant lemon wedge and carpeted with clothes. Leather boots, metallic sandals, platform flip-flops, and candy-colored jellies lay like rubble after an earthquake. Swimsuits, sarongs, gowns, tanks, shorts, hats, and a wrinkled heap of "borrowed" Ralphs had been tossed Ikea area rug–style.

"Ow!" Alicia whisper-shouted when one of her black-stockinged feet landed on something hard and cold . . . and gold! It was the RL charm on the scrunched-up GR bathing suit top. Once again it seemed to be mocking her, reminding her of what she had come to Spain for and what she had failed to get. It took all of Alicia's strength not to lift up the twins' red satin sleep masks and gouge their eyes out with the silver conchas on her RL Blue Label Mexican belt.

Suddenly, the muted shuffling sound of Nina dragging the garden hose across the roof made Isobel turn over in her carved wood canopy bed. And when Isobel turned, Celia turned. It must have been a psychic twin thing, because their matching kings were at least ten feet apart. Regardless, Alicia crouched down behind the burnt orange velvet chaise and held her breath, as if that might somehow reduce Nina's lumbering impact on the tiles above.

Figuring she was only seconds away from reaching her target, Alicia had no choice but to make her move. She hurried over to the bookless bookshelf and pressed EJECT on the twins' Sony stereo. The black machine, which was covered in makeup dust and gum wrappers, slide-offered its CD tray. Gently, Alicia placed the disc inside, grabbed the remote, and hurried to the door to wait for her cue.

All of a sudden, a rush of water trickled down the windowpane. Even though Alicia knew it was coming, the sight made her giggle. It looked so real! With renewed Spalpha confidence, she hit PLAY on the remote and speed-walked

down the corridor, victory-punching the sky to the boom-
ing sound of thunder. She'd taken it off the beginning of
ii!'s track and looped it over and over again—it seemed
only fitting that the twins miss their Rain in Spain audition
because of . . . the rain.

Mission accomplished!

Boo-woop. Boo-woop. Boo-woop.

Alicia didn't need Red Bull this time. Adrenaline—and her throbbing foot—had kept her up the rest of the night. Outside Alicia and Nina's bedroom windows, the morning sky was clear and the temperature was seventy-six degrees. But Celia and Isobel's windows would tell a very different story. . . .

"¡Va-mos!" She tossed a beaded green pillow at her cousin's head. "It's time. Good luck."

Nina leaped out of bed and bolted for the door.

"Wait! Aren't you going to wash the eye shadow off your face?" Alicia giggle-asked.

"Were they wearing their sleeping masks?"

Alicia nodded.

"Then they won't even notice."

Two minutes later Alicia heard the sound of Nina crawling back into her squeaky cot.

"Did it work?" she asked, rolling over to look at Nina.

"Perfecto!" Nina yawned and rubbed her eyes, leaving two skin-colored patches in the middle of her black-shadowed face. She looked like the opposite of a raccoon.

"What did you say?"

"I told them the auditions were postponed because of rain."

"And?" Alicia pushed, hoping her cousin hadn't forgotten the most important part.

"*Aaaand* they could take the day off because the guests were staying in their rooms." Nina fluffed one of her jewel-colored pillows and pulled her comforter over her double-Ds.

"Puuur-fecto!" Alicia kicked her legs in the air like a girl who had just outsmarted twin Spalphas. Her matador red–pedi'd toes seemed to be smiling back, congratulating her on a job well done. So did everything else in the room.

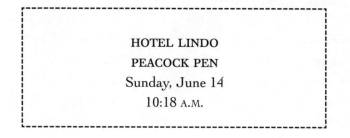

By Sunday morning, hundreds of wannabe video starlets with numbers pinned to their skimpy tops had lined up on the Lindo's back lawn, waiting to enter the audition tent. Apparently ii! had been asked to appear on Spain's highest-rated morning show—*Olé Mañana*—and couldn't be there, so he was leaving the decision in the hands of his trusted entourage. The preening girls were opposite of happy to learn of his absence but reassured themselves that they'd meet him when they won.

At least that was what Alicia heard when she and Nina passed by them on their way to the stinky bird pen behind the kitchen.

Esmeralda was waiting for them inside the mesh chain–enclosed sty, wearing bright yellow rain boots over black jeans and a khaki smock.

"Where's the leather?" Alicia teased, feeling particularly giddy thanks to the success of her Spalpha mission.

"It's bad luck to wear animal hide in an animal pen," Esmeralda said, like everyone already knew that. Then she reached into the pocket of her smock and scattered what appeared to be dead grasshoppers on the dirt. The birds flocked en masse, beaks at the ready. "As you can see, we have peacocks, peahens, and peachicks—"

"And pea-*ew*!" Alicia pinched her perky nose.

Nina burst out laughing. Then she pointed at a wet patch in the mud. "Look. Pea-pea!"

Alicia cracked up.

"Be serious!" Esmeralda squawked, wiping her dusty hands on her jeans.

Ay-ahhhhhh! Ay-ahhhhhh!

The male peacocks snapped their jewel-toned feathers shut while the peahens and peachicks scurried under their straw *palapa* for safety.

"I'm sorrrrrry I yelled," Esmeralda cooed at her beloved birds, then tossed them another handful of bugs.

Slowly they returned, pecking at the insects with their pointy beaks.

"After you feed the birds, please rake the pen clean of feces and—"

"*Poo*-cocks," Alicia whispered just loud enough for Nina to hear.

Their shoulders shook with suppressed laughter, but Esmeralda didn't notice. She was too busy reading a message on her pager, which had just buzzed loudly.

"They still make those?" Alicia whisper-asked her cousin.

Nina shook her head no.

"I must leave you now." Esmeralda took off her apron and tried to hook it over Alicia's neck.

"Ew, no way!" Alicia jumped back, swatting at the bug-filled pockets.

"*I'll* wear it," Nina volunteered a little too eagerly. Once the khaki ties were fastened around her neck and waist, the peacocks hurried toward her.

"I believe that once you get to know these lovable creatures, you will treat them kindly and feel shame for what you did to Bolero." Her eyes wandered to the far corner of the pen, where the peacock Nina had hit with ii!'s rubber jewelry hand was slumped against the wood fence, a white bandage around his tiny skull.

"Are you sure you trust us in here alone?" Alicia asked, hoping against all hope for a chance to audition. "Maybe we should come back when you have time to supervise."

"Esmeralda doesn't need to be here to supervise," the troll-like lady snickered, talking about herself in the third person. She plucked a fallen feather off the ground and hurried out of the pen as fast as her stumpy little legs would allow. "I always know what my chicks are up to," she added, before closing the gate behind her.

"I'll feed, you rake." Nina grabbed two fistfuls of dead bugs and threw them in the mud. "All done. Can we go now?"

"I wish." Alicia drew sad faces in the mud with the rusty rake. In the distance, "The Rain in Spain" was starting up again for the billionth time. Someone was auditioning. Someone other than her.

"ADM, come quick!" Nina shouted, surrounded by feasting peacocks. "This one's third eye is about to fall off."

"What?" Alicia dropped the rake and hurried to the center of the pen. Her sudden arrival did nothing to scare off the flock, thanks to the hundreds of dead insects scattered around their talons.

"Mira!" Look! Nina gripped the peacock's beak and turned it to face Alicia. A tiny round object was dangling from the center of his forehead. "His middle eye is about to fall off and we're going to get charged for it."

Stella McCartney's limited-edition peacock tee flashed into Alicia's mind. That bird had two eyes, not three. "I've never heard of a three-eyed bird." She giggled at her accidental rhyme.

"Tell that to these guys!"

Alicia forced her way into the bird circle and took a good look around. Nineteen birds and fifty-seven eyes stared back at her—an odd number if she ever knew one. "How is this possible?"

She leaned forward and took a closer look at the dangler. It looked exactly like the nanny cam her mother had hidden in the bread drawer when her father reluctantly went on a low-carb diet. She gasped. Was it possible that . . .

Alicia reached out and yanked the Minicam off the bird's blue head. The pin-size lens came off with ease, and the peacock fanned his undying gratitude.

"So that's how she knew what we were doing," Nina huffed, pulling a third eye off another grateful chick.

It all made sense now: Esmeralda had a bird's-eye view—literally—of her hotel and its guests. Alicia giggled at the idea, but brought her finger to her lips when she remembered they were still being watched.

Nina nodded in agreement.

Quietly they removed the cameras from all nineteen peacocks and dropped them in a pile of pea-poo.

"Ready to audition?" Nina asked with a toothy grin.

"In these?" Alicia pulled her sweaty uniform away from her even sweatier body.

Nina lifted off the apron and reached into her deep pockets. "No, in *these*." She held out two black bikinis with gold RLs hanging from the tops.

Alicia gasped, too speechless to ask the obvious.

"I took them this morning when I went to tell the twins the news." Nina beamed. "And I covered up the bulge in my pocket with the bug smock."

"¡Va-moooos!" Alicia threw her arms around her thieving cousin with newfound respect.

After a quick wardrobe change under the peacock *palapa*, Alicia and Nina ran across the field, holding hands and giggle-panting. Their big boobs, which had been packed into the small black triangular cups, were the only tip-off that the suits didn't belong to them. But, judging by the expressions of the people they passed, no one seemed to mind.

* * *

"Wait!" Alicia pant-shouted at G—or was it P or S—as he hung a TERMINADO sign in front of the now-closed green and white–striped tent flaps.

"Don't bother. Is over," a gum-snapping blonde tried to explain in her best English. "Winner is found."

"But we didn't get a chance," Nina shouted toward G/P/S.

"No one did," her pigtailed friend chimed in. "As soon as *they* showed up, it was over."

Celia and Isobel were off the to side, surrounded by envious wannabes and making victory-ii!'s with their fingers while they smiled for the press.

Without a single word of warning, Nina marched over and jumped in front of the cameras. "What are you doing here?"

"And why are you wearing my suits!" Alicia shouted loudly enough for the reporters to hear. It was important that *she* got credit for Celia's leopard-print bikini and Isobel's blue plunge-ruffled one-piece. It was essential that they knew she wasn't some SLBR, and that back home those cameras would have been on *her*.

The twins whipped their glossy brunette heads around, their photo-op smiles still intact.

"You stole *our* RLs, we steal yours." Isobel tossed back her bouncy blowout, and the cameras resumed their clicking.

"And nice try with the hoses, little sister," Celia chimed in. "The gardeners took them off the roof this morning, and poof! It stopped raining."

Alicia's shoulders slumped in defeat. The twins, being twins, were a double dose of Spalpha—two for the price of one. And only triplets could compete with that.

Alicia and Nina watched from their jail cell, otherwise known as the Toalla Hut, while the twins rehearsed their opposite of complicated dance routine with world-renowned choreographer Jocy O—a routine, by the way, that Alicia could have mastered in fifth grade. But Isobel and Celia, aka the Callas Sisters, as they had been dubbed by *¡Hola!* magazine, had been hard at work all week. And thanks to the paparazzi, everyone who read Spain's answer to *Us Weekly* knew it.

The pool deck was filled to fire-hazard capacity because cameras were set to roll in ten minutes, and ¡i! was finally going to make an appearance. But for Alicia, this was more about finding ways to make fun of the twins and find fault in the shoot so she'd feel better about not being part of it. Not that she'd ever *admit* that.

Finally, everything was in place for the video shoot to begin. The rain machine, the twins—even the unseasonably cool breeze and overcast sky, which, according to Fonsi, the director, worked perfectly with the moody-slash-gloomy feel of the video's story line.

After ten more minutes of waiting, Fonsi made a big

show of checking his watch before calling a huddle with G, P, and S. Celia and Isobel hopped up and down in their teeny denim cutoffs and fringed half-shirts, trying to stay warm.

"They think they're cold now?" Nina snickered. "Wait until that rain machine starts."

"Point." Alicia absentmindedly handed a blue towel to someone's pale arm and smile-thanked it for tossing a euro in the tip jar.

"They better get started before the real storm comes," said a familiar British accent.

"Hey, Nigel." Alicia allowed herself to grin. After all, the auditions were over. The ban on Brits was officially over.

"What's going on?" Nina asked when a hairy-chested man stepped onto the set. The crew quickly swiped some deodorant under his pits and brushed his body hair while a PA rolled a portable blue screen onto center stage.

Celia side-glanced at Isobel. *"¿Quien es el?"* She demanded to know who he was.

Isobel shrugged, then turned away in disgust.

"Yeah, who is that?" Alicia echoed.

"I hear ii! has a terrible flu and won't be able to shoot," Nigel whispered with the authority of a TMZ reporter. He leaned his elbows on the Toalla Hut's counter and took a sip from his bottle of Voss. "So they're going to use his stand-in and Photoshop ii! in later."

Alicia and Nina gasped in disbelief.

"Quiet on the set!" called Fonsi, waving his tan arms violently.

Someone quickly handed the stand-in an ice cream cone and positioned him between the twins.

"Walking on the pier, take one," Fonsi shouted. "Annnnnnd action!"

The music began and Isobel, Celia, and Hairy Stand-In began walking in place, the blank blue screen positioned behind them.

"A production assistant told me they were going to put an image of a Ferris wheel behind them so it looks like they're at an amusement park," Nigel explained.

"Stand by rain," Fonsi directed, pointing to the silver rain machine. "Cue the rain. Okay, Leon, drop the ice cream on your chest . . . *now*."

Leon did what he was told as a torrential downpour drenched the actors.

"Okay, girls, lick it off his che-ssssst . . . *now!*"

"Ew!" Alicia shouted.

"It's all hairy!" Nina screamed.

The twins must have felt the same way, because all they did was stare at the chocolate stream that was spilling down the stand-in's chest and pooling in his deep belly button.

"Cut!" Fonsi shouted, his temples pulsing. "You need to lick! LICK! Dry them off and reset for another take."

The twins pretended to gag while the crowd slowly returned to their sun cots and beach reads.

"Didn't I say you'd regret winning this contest?" Nigel winked.

Alicia looked at him—*really* looked at him—for the first time since they'd met. It felt like slipping on a great pair of wraparound D&G lenses after staring into the sun for hours. Her gaze could finally linger. And it did. . . .

"How do you know all of this?" she asked his clear blue eyes.

"ADM!" Nina gasped and covered her mouth. "ii!" she screech-shouted into her palm.

"*You* what?" Alicia asked her cousin, whose eyes were suddenly bulging from her skull.

"Quiet!" Nigel dropped his Voss and jumped through the window of the towel hut, ducking down by their flip-flopped feet.

"Not *me*," Nina whisper-shouted. "ii!"

Nigel looked up from the tiled floor, and Alicia quickly crossed her legs so he couldn't peer up her mustard-yellow dress. "I opposite of understand what's going on here."

"I am ii!," he said sweetly, not even *trying* to catch a glimpse.

"You are ii!?" Alicia ducked down to join him. Nina followed. "But you're . . . you're nawt even Spanish!"

"Shhhhhh." He waved his hand frantically in front of her open mouth.

Once she closed it, he continued. "I was lead vocal in a band back in Manchester until a talent scout offered me a contract to go solo. He said Spain was desperate for a pop star and asked if I wouldn't mind 'elping out, since we're all part of the same continent and all," he whispered. "So they airbrushed my face, Photoshopped my body, but kept my voice. *No one* knows."

"ADM, you're Fannish times ten!" Alicia blurted.

"I told you!" He smiled. "G, P, and S are my mother's nephews."

"And that rubber hand was—"

"A decoy."

"I can't believe you're ii!" Nina plucked a blond hair off his bare shoulder and stuffed it in her bikini top.

"What if your cousins tell?" Alicia asked, quickly calculating how many gossip points she could earn by breaking the news first.

"And give up all of this?" He gestured to the five-star resort outside the towel hut.

"I can't believe you're ii!," Nina muttered, tears rolling down her cheeks.

"Shhhhhh," Nigel smile-insisted.

"Why are you telling us?" Alicia asked, knowing full well she'd never be able to keep this from the Pretty Committee.

"Because I am hoping that *now* you'll finally agree to hang out with me." His crooked tooth and fair skin suddenly oozed quirky charm.

"We have jobs, remember?" Alicia insisted, shocking herself with the words she never thought she'd say—at least not in that order.

"Time for early retirement." Nigel stood, brushing off the seat of his slouchy, skull-covered board shorts. Obviously the trend was still very much alive in Europe.

"I can't believe you're ii!," Nina mouthed, a salty stream of mascara trickling down her face and into her cleavage.

Nigel handed her a towel.

"We have debt," Alicia explained.

"Not anymore." Nigel slapped his hands together like he was wiping off cake crumbs. "I paid it off."

"What?" Alicia jumped up and hugged him.

Nina cried harder.

"What can I do to repay you?"

"Keep my secret." He held out both of his hands. "And spend the afternoon sailing on my yacht. Looks like the sun is about to break through these clouds."

"Done!" Alicia grabbed hold of his hands firmly, cementing their pact.

She had never chosen loyalty over gossip before. But then again, she had never folded a towel, bonded with Nina, or decided that being an alpha was a lot less fun than just being herself.

"Can we go home and change first?" Alicia asked, rubbing her finger along the embroidered mop for the last time.

"*Please!* I insist on it." He chuckled his adorable Fannish chuckle.

Alicia, Nigel, and Nina held hands and walked proud as peacocks past the video shoot. Isobel and Celia were shivering while the hairy stand-in stiffly gripped his fresh new ice cream cone like the Statue of Liberty. Take two was about to begin.

Not just for the twins. For everyone.

Now that you know Alicia's summer secret,
you're another step closer to being **IN**.
In the know, that is. . . .

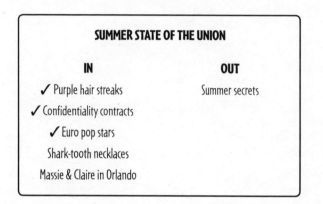

SUMMER STATE OF THE UNION

IN	**OUT**
✓ Purple hair streaks	Summer secrets
✓ Confidentiality contracts	
✓ Euro pop stars	
Shark-tooth necklaces	
Massie & Claire in Orlando	

Five girls. Five stories. One ah-mazing summer.

THE CLIQUE
SUMMER COLLECTION

BY LISI HARRISON

*Turn the page for a sneak peek
of Kristen's story. . . .*

THE CLIQUE
SUMMER COLLECTION

KRISTEN

THE BAXTERS' SUMMER RENTAL
WESTCHESTER, NY
Monday, July 18
11:43 A.M.

"Rate me."

"No."

"Come on, Ms. Gregory. Rate me."

"No."

"Kris-*ten*! Come on, pleeeease. You always rate Massie."

"No!"

"Just say a number."

"Fine. *Nine*."

"Ehmagawd! I'm a nine!" Ripple Baxter hugged the shell-frame mirror on the living room wall of her father's sea-inspired summer rental. "I knew this pink snakeskin headband was a must." She petted her deep-fried blond hair.

"Correction." Kristen sat on the floor, then placed her over-sweetened lemonade on the nicked surfboard coffee table. "It's not a rating. It's your *age*. You're *nine*." Kristen Gregory leered at Ripple from across the musty garage sale–furnished cottage. "And *nine* is the square root of eighty-one. Did you even know that?"

Ignoring her, Ripple turned to the side and examined her new outfit. A long, pale pink hoodie, meant to cover the hips, practically swallowed the top two-thirds of her short, muscular frame. Her knees could have easily been mistaken for extremely saggy boobs, had her purple rhinestone–covered flip-flops not been so close.

"Ripple, your dad is paying me to teach you math, and if you don't—"

"Ms. Gregory, he does not, not, *not* care about *math*." Ripple fluffed the dark lashes around her light brown eyes. "All he cares about are waves. He just wants someone to look after me so he can drive out to Long Island and surf. You're more like a tutor-sitter. Heavy on the sitter."

Funny. Lately Kristen felt *heavy* on everything. How could she not? While she sweated in a six-week summer school program, Massie was in the Hamptons, Alicia was in Spain, and Dylan was in Hawaii. Even Claire had left town. True, she'd gone back to Orland-*ew,* but that was better than tutor-sitting a bratty nine-year-old for eighth-grade wardrobe money. When would it be *her* turn to make memories? And when would Ripple stop with those annoying nickna—

"Actually"—Ripple flipped up her pink hood and checked her reflection—"the only thing you can teach me is how to *be* Massie Block."

"You could start by lowering that hood," Kristen blurted, then immediately angrily pinched her own leg for encouraging the little wannabe.

Ripple did what she was told, then reached into her Coach Heritage Stripe Swingpack knockoff and pulled out ten purple plastic bangles. Glued around them was a white price tag that said 5 FOR $2.00.

"Left or right?" She lifted her wrists. "WWMD?"

Kristen stood and shuffled across the uneven wood floor in Steve Madden cork wedges, her pleated Diesel denim mini swaying below her tight yellow ribbed tank. "Massie wouldn't do *either*!" She grabbed Ripple's soon-to-be-bangled wrists and pulled her back to the coffee table. "They're *H&M!*"

"Well, then, what *would* she do?" Ripple widened her light brown eyes in anticipation.

Kristen squeezed the gold locket Massie had sent her for her birthday—complete with a group photo of the Pretty Committee—and thought, *What* would *Massie do?* But, not being an alpha, Kristen wasn't completely sure.

"She would do her homework, *okay*?" Kristen lied, flipping open Ripple's glossy math textbook. "Now, if a carton of eggs was one-fifty yesterday and is fifty percent off today, how much are the eggs? A, a dollar; B, two twenty-five; or C, seventy-five cents?"

Ripple plopped down on the green and blue Hawaiian print–covered futon, annoyed. "Why won't you *help* me?"

"Because it's illegal to help a stalker." Kristen ran her hand along her stubbly calf, thinking that the best part of her pathetic day might be the leg-shave bath she had scheduled before bed.

"I am not, not, *not* a stalker!" Ripple whipped the bangles across the room. They bounced twice before settling into a cheap plastic heap.

"Then focus and answer the question!" Kristen shouted, grateful that they were the only ones home.

"Wait, I have a better question," Ripple sniffled. "If your three-week crush told you surf chicks were 'cute 'n' all,'" she air-quoted, "but that some sophisticated older girl named Massie Block was super hot, what would *you* do?" She stood and paced. "A, want to figure out the price of eggs; B, stay true to your surfer roots; or C, ask your dad to hire you the summer math tutor who just happens to be Massie's BFF?"

Kristen's stomach lurched. "You're using me for Massie info?"

Ripple smeared glittery pink drugstore gloss on her droopy bottom lip. "We're paying you, aren't we?"

Kristen felt dizzy. In that very instant, her entire world had just been turned upside down and dumped out like a giant handbag. Everything she'd held on to was gone. Being smart and athletic were the only two things she had that Massie couldn't compete with. No one on the Pretty Committee could.

And that made her special.

But who was she kidding? If the game Rock, Paper, Scissors were real life, it would be called Brains, Beauty, Brawn. And Beauty would beat Brains and Brawn every time.

Someone kicked the front door open. "Hello? Anyone home?"

A thick beam of sunlight seeped inside the dark cabin. A shirtless boy appeared in the doorway, as if summoned by God and delivered by angels.

"Dune?" Ripple ran to greet her brother. "What're ya doin' home?"

The thirteen-year-old surf star dropped his salty backpack and took off his white straw fedora. Blond hair the color of Baked Lays swung above his shoulders as he lovingly hugged his sister back.

Awwww.

"Coach kicked me off the team." He shrugged like someone who cared but didn't want anyone to know.

"Why?"

"The Atlantic was all lit up with phosphorescence. It was past curfew but I had to get in and ride."

"At *night*?" Ripple gasped, finally sounding like a nine-year-old.

"It was totally worth it." He rubbed his bare chest. "I caught a six-foot left and the water was glowing all green and everyone came out to watch and—" He stepped down the single step that led to the sunken living room and plucked a plastic Macintosh from a bowl of fake fruit on the rickety end table. "Who's this?" He tossed the apple in the air and caught it.

Kristen's skin stung the way it had when Principal Burns announced, to the entire school, that she had been named captain of the soccer team. He looked right at her, and she blushed like there were a hundred of him.

"Hey, I'm—"

"Oh, this is Ms. Gregory, my tutor." Ripple flirt-knocked the apple out of Dune's hand and giggled when it rolled across the floor.

"Stop calling me that!" Kristen reddened again, this time from rage. She was nawt going to be used and humiliated by a *nine*-year-old. As soon as their father came home, she was going to quit.

"Hey," he snicker-waved, unsure what to call her. "I'm Dune."

Kristen remembered seeing him at Briarwood's wave pool dedication ceremony last spring, but she'd been so distracted by her then-crush Griffin Hastings she hadn't noticed what a perfect hang-ten he was.

Ehmagawd! Kristen swallowed hard. Did she actually just think that? Whenever she had super-cheesy thoughts like *a perfect hang-ten,* she was entering crush mode. "You can call me—"

"Ripple!" Dune really looked at his sister for the first time since he'd walked in—from her pink headband straight down to her purple rhinestone flip-flops. "What are you getting tutored in? Looking like an OCDiva?"

Kristen silent-gasped. Was that what the surf guys called them?

"Trying," Ripple admitted shamelessly. "And please, from now on call me Rassie. Like Massie, but with an *R.*"

Dune hiked up his gold and brown slouching board shorts. "It makes more sense if you lose the *R.*"

Ripple burst out laughing, then whipped a stuffed starfish at his defined shoulders. For the first time in her life, Kristen envied a beige pillow.

"New York sucks." Dune tugged at the shark tooth necklace hanging around his neck, his mood shifting like the tides. "I can't believe I'm gonna be landlocked in Westchester all summer."

Just then a large, fit older man padded through the open door, his bare callused feet slapping against the dark floors like tap shoes. He clapped Dune on the shoulder. "Whose fault is that, son?"

"Dad!" Their shirtless chests slapped as they came together for a hug.

Brice Baxter smiled and ruffled his son's long straight hair. He wore camouflage trunks and a faded yellow DON'T WORRY, BE HAPPY baseball cap. "Now go grab your boards. We're going tanker surfing."

"But I just blew my hair!" Ripple whined.

Her father laughed, never suspecting that his tomboy daughter could have been serious.

"So, you're not mad I'm back?" Dune said to the fallen apple on the floor.

"Nah." Brice pulled the cap lower. "Your mother will be mad. But that's why we got divorced. That woman cannot go with the flow. I would have been mad if you passed up phosphorescent surf. Besides, the Tavarua trip is only six weeks away. Enjoy the break while you can."

Dune's warm brown eyes beamed respect and love for his father.

"You surf, Kristen?" Brice asked, the crispy corners of his hazel eyes scrunching with genuine hospitality.

"Um, no. I'm more of a soccer person," she said, making it perfectly clear that she was far from an OCDiva.

"Then tell your parents you won't be home for dinner."

He rested his arm on her sunburned shoulder. "Dune is gonna teach you how to surf."

Without hesitation, Kristen texted her parents, then followed the Baxters out to their blue Chevy Avalanche. Maybe she could give her job one more chance . . . for poor Ripple, of course.

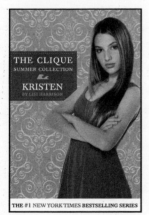

COMING TO DVD IN FALL 2008

ALWAYS KNOW THE CURRENT STATE OF THE UNION

REGISTER FOR UPDATES AT

THECLIQUEMOVIE.COM

Get all The Clique you crave online!

Visit Lisi Harrison at

www.lisiharrison.com

and

Win prizes, get downloads,
and chat with other Clique fans at

www.jointheclique.com

Welcome to Poppy.

A poppy is a beautiful blooming red flower
(like the one on the spine of this book). It is also
the name of the new home of your favorite series.

Poppy takes the real world and makes it
a little funnier, a little more fabulous.

Poppy novels are wild, witty, and inspiring.
They were written just for you.

So sit back, get comfy, and pick a Poppy.

poppy

www.pickapoppy.com